THE VAN DRAGGERS:

THE ACTIVITIES OF THIEVES IN THE LONDON AREA

To Sim

JOHN SWAIN

John Swain

Pen Press Publishers Ltd

First published in Great Britain
Pen Press Publishers Ltd
39-41 North Road
London N7 9DP

ISBN 1-904754-80-5

A catalogue record for this book is available
from the British Library

Printed and bound in Great Britain

Cover design by Jacqueline Abromeit

CONTENTS

FOREWORD

John Swain spent thirty years as a successful Police Officer, the latter part of that time as a Detective Superintendent, in the Criminal Investigation Department, at New Scotland Yard, tracking down active criminals in the London Area. Following his extensive experiences during those years, he decided to pass on to you the benefit of his considerable knowledge of the subject. In order to arrest criminals, catch them in the act, or thwart them in their nefarious activities, a Police Officer in particular must have some knowledge of what takes place on the other side of the fence, in the planning and execution of crime.

This book concentrates on the activities of those stealing from goods vehicles, known in the underworld as 'VAN DRAGGERS'. In addition, it gives you a 'Thieves' Eye View' of what takes place before, and even occasionally at the actual time of the offence. It should also be of great assistance to those engaged in the investigation and prevention of crime. They do not all get away with it!

There is little doubt but that those engaged in the haulage of valuable loads of the type mentioned in this book were later influenced into taking up the use of electronic safety and immoblizer systems to counteract this type of crime.

Perhaps, most important of all, it demonstrates in a quite positive manner how young people can be easily coerced into taking up criminal activities. More surprising, however, is the fact that even those whose parents go out of their way to guide them on the straight and narrow path of honesty and integrity are known to have been so influenced

At this point, the author would ask you to bear in mind that the writing of this book was prompted by an overall feeling of deja vu, experienced back in 1957. Then, as a recently promoted Detective Sergeant of the Metropolitan Police, he was posted to serve in Leman Street Police Station in London's East End, just a quarter of a mile from where he was born back in 1920.

His father had been a successful senior C.I.D. Officer in the Metropolitan Police who had retired from that Force in 1946, when the author had left the army and himself joined the Police. Consequently, then, serving in an area that had once been his home ground, the author was well briefed in what makes the young East Ender tick.

He had had plenty of close personal experience of their state of mind, from when he had attended school as the son of a detective who had recently arrested the father of one of his classmates. The result had always been the same. A fight. Thankfully, however, it was always a fair fight - one-to-one. Never did such incidents involve more than the angered and distressed son, and the author. There was never any outside interference or implement used. In fact, considerable respect for each other was learned, because these minor fracas usually took place in the school playground, and although there was always a duty Master in the area, he did not interfere at all, further than to insure that the boys shook hands at the end of the fight.

The author also found that his schoolmates were, for the most part, of an honest disposition. At the same time it was obvious that the parents of some of them were actively involved in crime of one sort or another. Respect for their father was very much in line with the respect held by the author for his father. They usually lived under the strict rule of 'just don't talk to or associate with policemen or strangers', in the same way that the author was obliged to accept the discipline of his father, a former Scots Guards Drill Sergeant. This was a brand of discipline that stood him in good stead, and may even have influenced him to join the Army when war was declared in 1939, and to join the Police Force in 1946, when he was demobilized from the army.

Sadly, some of his schoolmates became influenced by the successful criminal activities of their fathers. Some took up a life of crime, whilst others managed to learn from the fact that their own father had gone to prison, and stayed on the straight and narrow path of honesty and integrity.

In his then new position at Leman Street, the author was obliged to visit the scenes of many crimes and investigate matters as they presented themselves. These enquiries involved speaking to people living in the area, both parents and children. It was interesting work, in the course of which he was able to produce the necessary results to satisfy his superiors. The most interesting side of that work, however, to which he paid considerable attention, was his attempts to guide those who had just left school. From his worldly experiences he set his target as getting over the message of honesty and integrity to such youths. He could never be sure that he had got that message over, but contented himself with the thought that he had at least tried, and would continue to do so.

He was always very much aware of the numerous temptations open to young men as they left school. From having no pocket money, or the pittance given to the lucky ones by their parents, or earned doing a paper round, the school leaver soon learned that some of his older friends were making cash by stealing from shop counters and even from motor cars and vans. It was for this primary reason that the author had set his mind on guiding such youngsters away from crime, and to remain firm on the path of honesty and integrity. In fact, it became the moral behind the actual writing of this book.

GLOSSARY OF UNDERWORLD JARGON
(in chronological order).

Van Draggers: Criminals stealing valuable loads fromcommercial vehicles
Flog: Selling stolen property.
Malts: Speaking of local Maltese people.
Nick: To steal; the Police Station or Prison.
Drag: A motor car.
A Slaughter: A place for storing stolen property.
A Monkey: Five hundred pounds.
A Grand : A thousand pounds.
Jump Up: Stealing a vehicle or property from a vehicle.
Run In: Suitable place to drive in a vehicle loaded with stolen property.
A Firm: Group of criminal associates.
Sorted: Working out how to do a job.
Snout: Cigarettes,
The Law: The Police.
Stum: Saying nothing.
Look after: Paying for services.
Splash out: Spend more than normal.
Obbo: Keeping observation.
A Tun: A hundred pounds.
Bunny: Talk
Form: Previous convictions.
Hoisting: Shoplifting
Grass: To inform, or an Informer.

Ready eyed: ready to be stolen.
Hot wire: Byepassing the ignition to steal a vehicle.
G.B.H.: Grievous Bodily Harm.
Bung: Pay for services rendered.
Cozza: a Police Officer.
Bottle: Courage or guts

CHARACTERS
IN ORDER OF APPEARANCE

Mrs BURTON.
Charles BURTON
Dan JONES
Jim BAKER
TONY - Café owner
Peter GIBSBERG
Fast LOU
Ron - Driver.
Ted BEST
Fred STONE
Simon GABHOAN
Jack - Second driver.
Mr PEARSON
Mary MORRIS
George - lorry driver.
Bert HINCHCLIFFE
Detective Sergeant Jim MORRIS
Wally FISH
Foxy JONES
The Heavy Mob – The flying Squad
Detective Constable George BROWN
Detective Inspector Tom HUTCHINS
Detective Inspector Walter GRAHAM

CHAPTER 1
HOW IT ALL BEGAN

Myrdle Street, Whitechapel, is not the brightest area of the East End of London, but it was here that Charles Burton was born in March 1937. Despite the fact that this area is renowned as being the home of many involved in criminal activities, his father, a heavy lorry driver employed by a nearby haulage company, was regarded as a local pillar of honesty and integrity. Charles does not remember much about his father, who, he later learned, had joined the Royal Army Service Corps shortly after war was declared in 1939. Sadly, he was listed amongst those missing in action in the Eight Army El Alamein battles

As for the Burton home, it was situated in a second floor flat in a very old block of flats or apartments in Myrdle Street dating back to Victorian times. It was at least adequate for the family, consisting of two bedrooms, a living room, very small kitchen and a toilet. The cooking was done by gas and they did at least have electric lighting

The loss of her husband did of course add to Mrs Burton's responsibilities, as she was now harnessed with everything connected with bringing up young Charles. Thankfully, however, Dan Jones, the manager of the haulage firm that had employed his father, regularly added a few shillings to the little money in the family kitty, and encouraged Mrs Burton in the upbringing of her young son. Assistance that was well appreciated all round.

Mrs Burton did a great job bringing up young Charles, who soon proved himself to be quite a bright young lad, even at the infants school. This was followed by him slowly but surely progressing through his elementary school levels, and finally leaving school at fifteen years of age.

The loyalty of Dan Jones, whom Charles had got to know through his regular visits to the Burton home, is well worthy of a mention early in this story. Mr Jones had offered Charles a job as a junior clerk in the haulage company where his father had worked, when he left school. Young Charles was delighted to accept this offer, but stated quite firmly that his ambition in life was to follow in his father's footsteps, and become an accredited respected heavy goods driver.

Dan Jones was pleased to hear that Charles had this ambition. He told him that first he would have to obtain a driving licence, and that would mean taking driving lessons, an expensive project for one so young. Charles was fully aware of this, and proud of the fact that he would be the only breadwinner in the Burton household. Clearly he would have to wait until he was eighteen years of age, and would firstly have to somehow put some money aside in order to pay for the necessary tuition.

In his spare time after work, Charles spent most of his time in the local Maltese cafés with some of his old school chums They played good music, and his particular love during this period was the music and songs of Paul Anca. Although he enjoyed meeting his mates in these cafés, it did not take him long to realise that he could not afford to spend much time in them. He needed all of his spare cash to put aside for those driving lessons, because his allowance from his mother was very small indeed.

This initial shortage of cash guided him into confiding in his friend Jim Baker, and asking him what he could suggest. "Easy," replied the bold Jim. "Let's go into Boltons at Gardiners Corner, and pick up a few bits and pieces to flog to the Malts."

But Charles Burton, irrespective of the area in which he had been brought up, was not a thief. His mother had taught him to be honest, and he did not like the unsaid part of Jim Baker's suggestion. "Jim," he said, "you are trying to get me to come with you to Boltons store and nick some of their goods off the counters. I know some kids do this, but it is not for me."

"Jeez!" said Jim. "Look, if you want something, important you have got to go for it, it's most important that you to get the money for those driving lessons. Go for it Charlie, go for it!"

Having listened to this line of advice which he had no intention of taking, Charles bid his friend goodbye, left the cafe and walked home

He had no cash left, and could not see where he would get his tea money from for the following day. He had to do something, but what was there left to do? On arrival home, he put the question to his mother. Where or how could he raise that little extra money needed to put aside for the all important driving lessons he had set his mind on? She could not assist. She had no money except for her widows' pension, the pittance Charles gave her from his work, plus the occasional welcome hand-out from Dan Jones Therefore, she had been unable to put any money aside, or obtain work of any kind herself.

Charles did not sleep well that night. He was, as they say, 'bugged' by the thoughts brought out by his chat with

Jim Baker. The following morning, his worries continued. They even disturbed his concentration at work.
Then, after work, he decided to walk to Gardiners Corner, and have a quiet walk round Boltons Store.

Sure enough, there were plenty of interesting articles
on display, and the assistants did not seem very alert.
Yet the thought of actually stealing something gave
Charles a most peculiar and unhappy feeling inside. He
just could not do it. A voice in his ear brought him out
of his deep thoughts.

"So, you're not such a bloody goody-goody Charlie,
are you? You are checking up on what I said yesterday!
Now just watch me, you'll see, it's so easy, you'll be surprised." Now Charles was all for getting out of the shop
as quickly as he could, but he didn't like being called a
goody-goody. He decided to stay in the shop, but he was
not going to steal anything.

At the time when Jim had first spoken, he had been
standing close to a display of men's cufflinks. There were
many pairs of them displayed, secured to pieces of card-
board. Quite suddenly, Jim said in a loud voice, pointing
past the sales assistant to a man on the other side of the
store, "Look, Charlie, there's our old Headmaster over
there."

The sales assistant followed the direction that he was
pointing, but in the instant of her turning away, he had
picked up two pairs of cuff links, put them in his pocket,
and carried on talking about the so-called headmaster.
They then moved to another counter where a number of
small tools were displayed. "I could do with one of those
small screwdrivers," said Jim. He then repeated his previous action by calling Charles' attention to another man,
who he indicated in a loud voice, saying, "That's our old

Headmaster again."

Once again the sales assistant turned away and, quick as lightning, Jim scooped up one of the attractive looking insulated screwdrivers. Charles had had enough, and said so. Turning away from his friend, he said "I'm off Jim, this is not for me."

That evening, Charles made for his favourite Cable Street café for a chat with some of his mates, and to listen to some more music. He was enjoying himself until Jim came in at about nine o'clock. He got up to leave the café, but Jim came over to him and gave him two one pound notes. "If you are going home, take this and put it to one side for your driving lessons," he said. "There's plenty more where that came from, and you don't have to steal anything, just leave that side of matters to me. I have to have someone with me to do what I have to."

At that time, Charles .was only earning three pounds eight shillings a week. Two pounds was more than he could ever hope to put to one side in one go. He was tempted. I wonder how many young men have been turned into criminals by just this manner of approach. My experience tells me that this was far from being an isolated incident. It also confirms my conviction that parents should be more watchful over their youngsters at this age. Watchful of them bringing home items that they say they have found or won! Also of having a little more pocket money than they should be expected to have.

After work, two days later, Jim was waiting outside the company premises for Charles to leave, and they headed for the same Boltons Store. The first stop was the counter where some scarves were on display. Whilst examining some of these, Jim suddenly indicated a so-called 'relative' of his over on the other side of the store.

As the assistant turned to look, Jim picked up a scarf which he pushed down inside his zip jacket.

This was too much. It was so obvious. Surely the store staff were not that stupid?

The boys then moved towards the tool counter. Once there, Jim went into the same routine, indicating a mythical figure on the far side of the store. Incredibly, the assistant looked again and Jim helped himself to two of the same screwdrivers he had previously stolen. Turning to Charles, he said, "No bother. We can sell these without any trouble."

Charles indicated it was time to go because he felt that surely someone was going to recognise them before long. Jim was finally induced to leave the shop.

As they approached the exit, Jim said, "If anyone ever tries to stop us, ignore them and just walk away. Whatever you do, don't run. Some of these store detectives are a bit fast. Just walk into the traffic, we are far more nimble than those blighters."

At that moment, he pushed the store door open, and they both stepped out on to the pavement. Charles did not see what happened next, he just wanted to get away from that store. Then he realised that he was walking towards his home, alone. Looking back, he saw Jim up against the shop front with two large men talking to him. What should he do? This was something they had never discussed.

Charles walked to the other side of the road, and back towards where his friend was detained. Clearly, he could do nothing, but felt that he should at least let Jim see that he had not just run off and left him. From about two hundred yards away, he watched the two men, one holding Jim against the front of the shop, the other going through his pockets and showing Jim the scarf that had been under his jacket.

After about twenty minutes the two men led Jim away across the High Street, down Leman Street, and into Leman Street Police Station. This was the first time Charles had witnessed such an awful event, and he was most worried about what he could do to assist his friend. He went to his usual café, but did not mention what had happened to anyone, even to Tony the boss. In his mind he was satisfied that he was not really responsible for what had happened, but his inner feelings were telling him loud and clear that he must not get involved again with Jim in such activities.

Finally, at about nine o'clock, he left for home, a little later than usual. On his arrival at his flat in Myrdle Street, he found that his mother was near to tears. She was worried about where he had been, and felt that he must have had an accident.

Once again, Charles did not sleep well, Most unusual! He usually slept so soundly and was never disturbed at night. He was quite sure that his friend had been arrested, but could do nothing to help him. How glad he was that he had not been a direct party to the thefts. At the same time he nevertheless felt sure that in the eyes of the law, perhaps he was just as guilty as Jim, as his helper or accessory. He vowed that he would not go to Boltons again unless it was to make a genuine purchase.

The following day, Charles found great difficulty in concentrating on his work. He could not get Jim or the Boltons incident out of his thoughts. Had they kept him in the station overnight? Would he be taken to that Police Court in Arbour Square that day? Questions, questions, questions. They kept coming, but he had no answers.

At Tony's café that night, Jim was the main attraction. He had told everyone what had happened, and even congratulated his friend and 'accomplice', which was a great relief to Charles. According to Jim, Charles had not panicked, he had just walked away as if nothing had happened. "What an actor," he said. "If he had made a fuss, the two of us would have been nicked instead of just me." Now at least he could call on Charles again on his next step into the man's world.

Charles listened intently and nodded, but at the same time he told those present that he had no intention of ever going out with Jim nicking things from shop counters again. He was quite surprised to find that Jim had plenty of cash with him that evening, and after ordering a pie and chips, Jim asked Charles to sit with him and explained that he now had to find something more lucrative to do. He insisted that there was plenty of honest cash to be had, but he needed an assistant.

Charles tried to explain that he had done nothing, but Jim would not listen. The assistants had not seen Jim take anything, that visit had gone off 'as sweet as a nut', as he used to say. It was his fault he had been nicked. "That bloody scarf I put under my jacket was hanging out, and that was why the store detectives pulled me."

This was quite a cosy chat, and Charles came away from the café that night thinking what a great chap Jim really was. If he was going to get involved in anything, it would have to be with Jim. He was so calm, even if he was a thief, there was no doubt about that; and he had a few bob to spend as well. So, whatever he was up to, it certainly seemed to pay off. He had insisted that whatever he got involved with, Charles would be doing honest work for which he would be paid.

At this time, work for Charles seemed to go on at the

same pace. He still had his eyes on becoming a Heavy Goods Driver, but his savings, such as they were, would go nowhere near the costs of the lessons required just to get an ordinary driving licence. Then of course, with his nineteenth birthday coming up, he felt very frustrated.

One evening at Tony's café, Jim told Charles that he had arranged for him to have some private driving lessons from a friend who was a car dealer and had his own 'drag'. "How much was this going to cost?" asked Charles.

"Don't worry about that, I'll see to it," said Jim. "I have some good jobs in mind, and will need a driver. You are just the bloke for me. You are cool, and don't panic. You've proved that already. You come here Saturday afternoon after work, and I will have my friend here with me."

Charles was at Tony's café at one o'clock that Saturday afternoon, and was introduced to Peter Ginsberg, who had a Morris Oxford Saloon motor car in a nearby street. After the introductions, Jim and Charles went to the car with Peter, and got in. Peter immediately started to tell Charles just what he was doing with the controls to get the car moving; in fact, for a few minutes, he gave quite a running commentary of his actions, while Charles attempted to keep pace.

Suddenly, Peter stopped the car, got out and, coming round to the passenger side, told Charles to get into the driver's seat. Thereafter, under the close instruction and supervision of Peter Ginsberg, Charles drove the vehicle round quiet streets for nearly an hour.

Finally, Peter and Jim both announced that there would be no difficulty in teaching Charles to drive a car, because he had it in him. Then Peter told Charles to stop the car. This he did, and received a hearty slap on the back from Peter, who announced, "You're OK, Charlie boy, you're a bloody natural."

These lessons went on regularly for about a month. The strange thing was that each lesson seemed to be in a different vehicle. Charles mentioned this on one occasion to Jim, but all he would say was that Peter was a dealer and had a lot of cars.

Charles finally managed to pass his driving test, and obtained a full licence. He felt that he had one foot on the ladder to reach his ambition, but realised that he would have to get in plenty of driving practice first. The problem was that he did not have a motor car, and could not see any possibility of being able to purchase one himself for many years. He mentioned this sore point to Jim, who just chuckled and said, "Leave that to Peter and me. Between us we will see that you get all the practice you are ever likely to need. Trust us Charlie. We know what we are doing."

Charles was taken to a railway arch just off Back Church Lane in Aldgate, where Jim showed him a small van. "Do you think you could drive that?" asked Jim. Charles got in, and after doing all the things that he had been taught, adjusting the seat and driving mirrors, drove it out of the arch. "Great," said Jim. "We have a little job to do over the river, and Peter wants you to drive the van of a friend of his, back to the arch."

They then walked to Tony's café and met Peter. "I'll go and get the drag," said Peter, and left the café. He returned a few minutes later. Jim and Charles both got into the Morris Oxford Saloon, the car that Charles had first seen, and were driven off.

"Tooley Street," said Jim. Along Cable Street, a few turns and then left over Tower Bridge, turning right at the foot of the Bridge and along a few hundred yards where they stopped.

"Our friend has not arrived yet," said Peter. The trio then settled down for a nice smoke and chat. Charles could not work out what was happening, but said nothing. He was at least getting on well with his driving.

After about twenty minutes, a blue van about the size of the one Charles had driven earlier stopped outside a warehouse in Tooley Street. The driver got out and went into the premises. "I won't be a minute," said Peter. He walked along to the van, stopped by it and gave the thumbs up signal, then opened the van door and climbed in. Jim then said, "That is one of Peter's vans, he will want you to drive it back to our railway arch in a few minutes. You go over towards him, and when he tells you, get in and drive it back over the bridge. We will follow on and open up the arch for you so you can drive straight in."

Doing exactly as asked, Charles walked over towards the van. Peter got out of the cab, motioned to Charles to join him, said, "I'll see you over the river at the 'Slaughter'," and walked off towards Jim. Charles got into the van and drove it away, turning over Tower Bridge and on to the railway arch in Back Church lane. Jim was waiting for him. The arch was open, and he drove in as directed. Peter had by this time driven the other van away.

Charles climbed out of the cab and walked over to Jim. "A great job," said Jim. "Let's see what we have now." With that he opened the back of the van with some keys. Inside the van was a conglomeration of what looked like fairground prizes, all nicely boxed and wedged in such a position that they did not rattle or break.

"That's your first big job Charlie," said Jim. "It should earn us both a hundred quid a piece.

"I thought this van belonged to Peter," said Charles."

"It belongs to the three of us now," replied Jim.

The Van Draggers

The van was unloaded, and the contents stacked up in one corner of the arch. "What is the next move?" said Charles.

"The next move is yours, Charlie, when it is dark take this van and leave it up in Golders Green, or somewhere up that way. Then forget all about it. Just one thing: take these old gloves, wear them, and use them to wipe any fingerprints off the steering wheel or anything else you may have touched. I will see you at Tony's either tonight, or tomorrow evening. With that said, Charles made his way to Myrdle Street, deep in thought, and wondering just what he would be expected to do next.

After a pleasant tea at home, Charles bid his mother goodbye for the evening, and returned to the railway arch. He drove the stolen van to Golders Green, and left it in a side road near the Kings Arms public house. Throughout the journey, Charles was turning over in his mind the activities of the day. Something was not right. He had seen Peter go over to the van and produce something like a steel ruler from his inside jacket pocket and pass it down between the side window of the van and the door, which had then opened. Then, on the return to the Back Church Lane Arch, Jim had asked him to just drive the van away, and abandon it up in north London, and to be sure to clean off any marks, such as fingerprints.

He was very unhappy. He was being used, but he had at least had free driving lessons, and his driving was improving from day to day.

Charles made his way by bus back to Cable Street and Tony's café. Peter and Jim were both there, and glad to see him. "Everything OK?" asked Jim.

"No problem," replied Charles. They chatted away for quite some time after the initial greeting. It seemed that there was a further job that they wanted Charles to do for them..

Then Jim handed Charles an envelope stuffed full of something. "Don't open it now," he said. "That's for you, and look after it. There's more where it came from, and I believe we should be getting some more interesting work soon."

Charles had the distinct feeling that he was being drawn into a very lucrative but highly illegal operation. He was in no doubt that Peter had in fact broken into and fixed the ignition of the van he had driven back to the arch, and on to North London. Everything seemed so well organised, however, so why should he worry? He was driving legally now, and had a proper driving licence.

This all seemed too good to be true. Such a small job yet, from the feel of that envelope, such a lot to be earned. Charles was secretly enjoying the thrill of this new line of work. The envelope was burning a hole in his pocket. He had to open it up. He went into the toilet, and after locking the door he examined what he had.

One hundred pounds in five pound notes! Not a bad start. He was beginning to like his new lifestyle. On his way home that night, his main thoughts were concentrated on what he was going to do with the hundred pounds that were still burning a hole in his pocket. He had to hide it somewhere, where no other person would find it, particularly his mother. If she found it she would have a fit. He had heard one of the lads talking in the café who said that the best place to hide anything like cash or jewellery was behind the back of an unused fire. It has to be a fire that is never used. Apparently if you put your hand up the chimney, touching the back of the flue, you come to a gap that is not far up. Down behind that gap an open space goes back and down to about the level of the actual grate. To Charlie, this had sounded a little far fetched at the time, but now, when he actually had something to hide, it came to him as something of a relief.

On his arrival back at Myrdle Street, his mother was in bed asleep. He knelt down by the fireplace that was packed with Christmas paper and odds and ends like a few fir cones, and a small log. He put his right arm up the chimney and sure enough found the gap. He then found a piece of string, tied a pencil to it and lowered it down the hole behind the fire until it reached the level of the grate. This had to be the ideal hiding place.

The next stage was to find a plastic bag. Into this he put the treasured and valuable envelope containing the money. He tied the string round the top of the plastic bag, and at an estimated length to the depth level of the grate, he secured a piece of coathanger wire formed into an 'S' shape. This he hooked over the edge of the gap up the chimney, after lowering the plastic bag to the bottom. Siting back he felt very proud of himself.

That fireplace had never to his knowledge been used for heating. The flat was heated by an old paraffin Valor stove, which was quite adequate for their needs. In any event, there was no place where coal or coke could be stored in the flat except underneath the food cupboard or larder, such as it was. Charles had heard his mother say on one occasion that she would never keep coal, with all of the dust that goes with moving it, so near to the food.

After rearranging the odds and ends in the fireplace, Charles retired to his bed, feeling very proud of his efforts. He was the only person who now knew where his money was hidden, and it would remain that way. If there was another job, and it sounded as if there would be, that is where he would put his share. He slept very soundly that night.

Arriving at work the following morning, Charles made his way to the manager's office. He explained that he was not entirely happy as a clerk, and wanted to get some driving experience. He explained that he had taken a driving course, and produced his driving licence to back up his claim. Dan Jones was pleased and said, "Do you think you can drive the firm's delivery van Charles?"

CHAPTER 2
ADVANCING IN CRIME

The van was about the same size as the one Charles had driven only a few days earlier. This should cause him no trouble at all and he told Mr Jones that he was quite sure he would have no difficulty driving it. "Right," said Mr Jones, "let's take it out for a run."

The van was parked in the company yard that opened into Cannon Street Road. Charles was given the keys and got into the driver's seat. The manager got in beside him, and he drove into the road. "We have a small delivery in Epping," said Mr Jones. "Do you know your way there?" Charles had no idea of the way to Epping, and said so, but pointed out that if Mr Jones directed him he would be able to get there quite safely.

The result was that Charles impressed his boss with his driving ability. He was told that he would now be the van driver for small deliveries, and when there was a valuable load to be collected or delivered in the heavy lorries, he could go along as the driver's mate. This would give him the opportunity to study routes of the heavy goods driving operation, and perhaps in due time he would be sent on a course and obtain the required heavy goods licence. Charles was elated. This was more than he could ever have expected.

With his new job as a van driver and drivers mate, Charles' wages increased just a little, though he now found it difficult to get down to Tony's café as often as before. He enjoyed talking to the experienced drivers whenever possible. There was so much to learn about traffic, regulations, and the law with regards to heavy goods vehicles.

On one trip to Tony's, Jim mentioned that he was surprised to see him, and asked what he was doing. Charles explained that he now had a chance to get into heavy goods driving within the firm and was paying more attention to his work. Jim patted him on the back, and said, "You are doing the right thing, Charlie. Peter and I know you are a good driver, and if you get the heavy goods ticket, we will really be in business."

Looking Jim square in the face, Charles turned to his friend and said, "Now Jim, we're mates, but you get this straight: I will never do anything that hurts my firm, they have been very good to my old lady, and me. Forget it."

Jim looked hurt, and went on to explain that with the amount of the work they had in mind, the fact that he was a respected heavy goods driver in regular employment was something that would assist them in their future operations. Furthermore, the next time he gave him an envelope, it would be for a 'monkey' or a 'couple of grand'. The thought of receiving such sums was enough to make Charles think very deeply about his future. He was, however, quite satisfied in his own mind that he would not do anything to hurt his firm.

Charles continued with his work as van driver and driver's mate. He was enjoying this type of work, and the freedom it gave him to travel around the capital. He was even allowed at times to drive the heavy lorries when they had been on a long run and the driver was a little tired. This was quite unofficial, of course, and he was sworn not to let anyone know what he had done.

With the summer holidays approaching, Jim was anxious to know what time Charles would get off work for the holiday period. "I get a fortnight," said Charles, "but what is the interest?" he asked.

"Peter is working on a big 'jump up' down in Kent, somewhere near Paddock Wood, and we are going to need your help. I am now working on the 'slaughter', but should have that sorted in a few days."

Charles was quite mystified by Jim's reply, and said, "What the hell are you talking about? What's this 'jump up' business, and what on earth is the 'slaughter'?"

Jim sat back and roared with laughter. "Charlie my old mate!" he said. "Our firm is the three of us - you, me, and Peter - and you've already done a jump up job for our firm when you jumped up into the driving seat of the van down in Tooley Street, and drove it back to our 'slaughter' - the arch, that's our slaughter. But it only holds a small vehicle. What we are going to need this time is a big shed or barn - in fact a run-in slaughter, where you can drive straight in and be safe from outside eyes."

Charles was still a little concerned as to just what was going on, and said so. He was impressed by the sums of money he might earn, but could not see how it could be worked out accurately, and in advance. "You are always checking up on me," said Jim. "You checked up on me in Boltons a few years back, remember? Now remember this: our firm is the three of us, you, me, and Peter, and we rely on each other. Peter finds the work. Remember? He found that van you drove from Tooley Street. He then fixes the ignition so you can drive it away. I find the slaughters, like I found the arch, and I find the buyers for the gear we nick. All you have to do is jump up into the driving seat, and drive the vehicle to the slaughter. Then leave the rest to us. Your share will be given to you as soon as we have some funds, and we split even, after expenses have been paid."

Charles was given the first two weeks of August as his summer holiday, with holiday pay in advance, which he had not expected. He returned home and gave the bulk of his money to his mother. That evening at Tony's café he told Jim the news. "Great," said Jim, "we should have something in the next few days. The job is nearly sorted, so keep Wednesday free, that's the favourite day as I see it."

On the Tuesday evening, Jim was in great form. "Meet Peter and me here at nine in the morning, it's on," he said. Nothing further was said, and they parted company. Once again, Charles did not sleep too well that night, after having to spend a long while making excuses to his mother for what he was going to do the following day.

He was still up bright and early, however, and after a quick breakfast, made his way to Cable Street to meet his mates. Jim, who was sitting in the front of the Morris Oxford with Peter, opened the back door for Charles, and told him to get in. "We're going for a ride in the country," said Jim. "Can you drive a big A.E.C?"

"I can drive most things" replied Charles. They then made their way over Tower Bridge to the Old Kent Road. They continued in a south easterly direction out into the Kent countryside. Nothing was said during this journey until they started to drive south along the main A21 road. Peter then took up the conversation. "We are going to a big lay-by near Paddock Wood. There I will indicate a big one that you can get in and drive away. You follow me, that's all you need to know."

Sure enough, they arrived at a lay-by with some very large vehicles in it. Peter gave Charles a set of keys and, indicating a large covered vehicle, said, "That's the one, it belongs to a friend of mine. You get in and drive off, we will be in front of you, and we won't lose you."

Charles got out of the car and made for the big A.E.C. He unlocked the driver's door with the keys and made himself comfortable in the driver's seat. The cab was still warm. He switched on the engine, which thankfully answered up immediately, then went into first gear and he moved off smoothly. He followed the Morris Oxford on to the A21, then turned left in the direction of Goudhurst. The guiding vehicle was slowing down so Charles followed suit, then as it turned up a lane he followed.

At this stage, Charles had one big worry. Would the big vehicle be able to make it along these narrow byways? After about a quarter of a mile, he was relieved to find his guide stopping at a farm entrance. Here Jim got out of the Morris Oxford and, standing on the running-board beside Charles, guided him over to a large barn that Peter was in the process of opening. Peter then drove the car inside and guided Charles to park alongside him in the barn.

The job was not over yet. Throwing back the canvas covering, Jim called Charles to stand below him in the barn and take from him packing cases that he lifted from the lorry. These contained cigarettes, thousands of them. What a haul! They were all stacked up in a corner of the barn, and then covered over with the tarpaulin from the back of the lorry.

Jim then called, "That's it Charlie. Now get rid of the lorry. I suggest you take it back down the lane and then turn left. If you keep going straight, you will end up somewhere in the Canterbury area. We have a couple of hours before the balloon goes up. You drive on, we'll follow you and pick you up when you've left the vehicle in some parking area."

This was all too easy. Charles drove off as directed, and finally landed up at Chartham, just outside Canterbury, where he parked up the lorry in a large public house car park. He cleaned up the steering wheel and door handles, and got back into the Morris Oxford with his mates.

It was a very happy group who drove home that night. At Westerham, they stopped in the car park of a public house near the General Wolfe memorial statue, had a good drink and a handsome meal. Life was beginning to look good for our Charles. He was enjoying the thrill of the work and the company he was now keeping, and had forgotten his misgivings.

Back at Cable Street, Jim said, "Can you make it in the morning Charlie? We still have a lot of work to do." It was agreed that the trio would all meet at Tony's café in the morning, although Jim did not say what would be happening then.

Charles arrived at nine o'clock the following morning, as requested, and once again got into the back of the Morris Oxford. The next stop was the railway arch, or local slaughter. Jim opened up, and told Charles to get the van out. This he did, and Peter drove the car inside. With the three of them in the van, Charles was directed to drive the van back to the farm in Kent. There they drove into the barn, and commenced loading packages of cigarettes into the van. When the van was full, the amount of packages still in the barn seemed to be about the same. There were certainly a lot of cigarettes to be got rid of!

After tidying up the barn and covering over the loot, the trio made their way back towards London. There was no stopping at Westerham this time, it was work in hand that had to be attended to. "What work?" asked Charles.

"We are going to get rid of this snout," replied Jim. "Peckham is the next call!"

Peckham it was. At the first public house they stopped at, Jim apparently knew the licensee, and went inside. He returned a few minutes later, and stood by the back of the van. Then next thing was that the cellar flap opened upwards, and a voice from below shouted, "I'll have six." With that Jim opened up the back of the van and took six packages out and lowered them down to the licensee in the cellar. He then entered the public house, and came back a few minutes later with a nice roll of bank notes in his hand.

Peter, this time directed Charles to drive to another public house in Peckham. This time he entered the premises, and Jim stood at the rear of the van. Within a few minutes the same procedure was adopted. The cellar flap opened up, and from below a voice said, "I'll take the lot, sling them all down." Jim accompanied by Peter then emptied the van and lowered all of the remaining packages down to the licensee. Peter then went back inside the premises, and came out this time with his pockets full of bank notes. Business was good.

"Back to Kent!" commanded Jim. They returned to the farm, and once again entered the barn and filled up the van. This time it was clear that half of the stolen load had been moved. Back to our slaughter now," said Jim. "We will get rid of this lot in the morning."

Thus the next stop was at Back Church Lane, and to the railway arch. Here they left the van and contents inside, and made their respective ways home. During the journey, Peter had counted out the cash he had taken from the publican for the cigarettes and given Jim his share. "Jim looks after the cash," said Peter. "There are expenses though: the farmer wants his rent for the barn, the lorry driver wants his whack for giving us his lorry, and keeping out of the way before reporting it missing. There are many things that have to be attended to, and Jim sees to all of that. We only want one face known and that is Jim's."

During the next three days they were busy indeed. The barn was finally emptied and all the packages sold to publicans known to Jim and Peter. There were no hitches or questions. Each call or stop was done in broad daylight, and the same routine applied. One of the team went into the public house, then returned. The cellar flap would open and the goods would be lowered into the cellar. There was nothing unusual about the deal and to the ordinary outsider who may have seen the van being emptied, it looked like an honest and correct business deal.

When all the loot had been disposed of, Jim and Charles met one evening in Tony's café. This was not a chance meeting; Jim had been waiting for Charles to turn up as usual. "Peter has been nicked," said Jim, "but don't worry, they can't have anything on him. It seems the driver of that lorry said he was in the pub near where he parked his lorry, having a meal. Then when he left at closing time in the afternoon, his lorry had gone and he telephoned the police. As a result of the police enquiries, they found that the driver had got into our drag - the Morris Oxford - with an unknown man some days earlier."

It turned out that the police had traced the car from the number that someone had taken, and now they were trying to say that the lorry driver gave his lorry and load away to Peter. The trouble was, there was no saying just what the lorry driver might say next. Jim then gave Charles a bag containing some bagels. They were warm, and smelled wonderful. "Take these home to your mother," said Jim, "but don't let her unpack the bag, there's a grand in there."

Charles took the still warm rolls home to his mother. She was both surprised and delighted. Jim unpacked them and placed them in the kitchen cupboard for her. While doing this, he found that there was a large envelope filled with bank notes in the bottom of the bag.

That night, Charles took down a book to read, something he had not done for some while. He settled down to read until he was sure his mother was in bed and asleep. He then went to the fireplace, lifted the soot covered bag out of the chimney, put the latest envelope into the plastic bag and lowered it back behind the fireplace as before. Then, after a good wash, he retired to bed - perhaps not to sleep, but to pray a little, as he was very worried about the arrest of his friend Peter.

The following morning, after a good breakfast, Charles walked down to Cable Street. As he passed the arch in Back Church Lane, he noticed that the padlock was not in place. Pushing the gate open, he entered and found Jim tidying up inside the van. "I'm glad you have come along," he said. "I'm checking up to see if there is anything lying about that should not be here, like bits from those snout' boxes, that could drop us in it. Also I am glad you have come along because there are a few things that we should get straight."

They sat down on a bench in the corner of the arch. Jim then gave Charles a scrap of paper with some writing scrawled on it: the name Fast Lou, followed by a telephone number. "That's our safety net," said Jim. "If ever you are pulled in by the law get hold of Mr Lewis, we know him as 'Fast Lou', because he works very fast, and immediately. He is also a bloody good brief. Don't say anything until he arrives; wherever you are, only talk in his presence. The Law have got to let you have a telephone call, make sure you get in touch with him. Day or night you can always contact him through that number. Try to remember it, don't get caught with it on you."

Charles had been worried about quite a number of things of late, particularly since he had been told there was trouble afoot regarding the lorry he had moved, firstly to the farm, and then to the pub car park outside Canterbury. He was also worried as to how Jim should know about any trouble. Now it was beginning to take shape. The conversation went on for quite some time. Peter had made contact with Fast Lou, who did what he felt best, then just waited. Lou knew that if all was not well, Jim would be in touch with him as usual. As a result of Jim's enquiry, all Mr Lewis had said was, "I'm was busy down in Kent, just leave it to me."

By this system, there was no flap or panic. Lou would look after the legal matters, and Jim and Charles would be informed if anything had to be done. It seemed that Jim had put together quite a smooth operation, but what worried Charles most of all was how this Lou would get in touch with him if there was anything to worry about, or do. It seemed that the most important thing to re-member was not to make himself busy by going to a Mag-istrates' Court and asking questions, as in the case of Peter, or the lorry driver. If he did, the Law would be on to Jim or Charles straight away, and they would find them-selves being stopped in the street and dragged in for ques-tioning. If anything had to be done, Lou would make contact with Jim through Tony's café, and that was why the café had to be the regular stopping place.

Charles was still a little worried, and asked what should be done next. The reply was simple. Do nothing. If anything had to be done, Lou will let it be known through Tony's café. It was decided that the waiting time would be spent in the arch sprucing up the van, not using it, but having it ready for use at a future date.

There was no movement, or information about the situation for some while. During this time, Charles real-ised that his holiday period was running out. He would soon be back at work, and not able to become involved in anything to do with 'the business'. He reported back to his work place in Cannon Street Road, and got on with whatever job was given to him to do.

On the evening of his first day back at work, Charles went down to Tony's café, and to his surprise found Pe-ter sitting there chatting to Jim. The conversation was hushed, but it seemed that someone had seen the lorry driver get into Peter's car and taken the number. It had all come out when the Law started making their enquir-ies about the stolen lorry and load. Peter had correctly registered the ownership of the Morris Oxford, and it was only a matter of minutes before the police were round his flat making enquiries.

John Swain

They took him and the car down to Kent, and grilled him there. Peter admitted that he had been in the area, but denied any suggestion put to him by police. He had been allowed to make a telephone call, and Fast Lou had arrived at the Police Station and sorted matters out. The result was that Peter had been bailed to return to the Police Station the following Monday, and would do so with Mr Lewis. There was nothing to worry about.

As for the Morris Oxford, Peter had told the police that he had received a wonderful offer for the car from a friend who was a dealer in Warren Street, and had in fact taken it there earlier that day for sale. He had taken a little Beetle in part exchange, but would only use it for runabout purposes, and would not use it on 'business'. In any event, he felt that it was high time he had another drag, for general use.

As to the lorry driver, as far as could be made out, he was 'stum', and had not been paid or said anything out of place. The Law had been unable to break him, and he was also on bail. Peter was in touch with him through a friend, who had told him that everything was under control, and that was the end of that. Finally, Jim announced that he would 'look after' Fast Lou and the driver when the time was right.

The little meeting finally broke up at about eleven o'clock that evening, and it was decided that they would meet most evenings for a cup of tea and a chat, just in case anything else of interest turned up in the meanwhile. Before they parted, however, Jim looking straight at Charles grabbed his hand, and said, "Charlie my old mate, you have a few bob now. Whatever you do, don't start spending it. The Law will be watching for that sort of thing. Splashing out you will get nicked and that's for sure, so wherever your loot is, leave it there, and live on your wages, even if it hurts. Don't even tell your old lady you have had a win at the dogs, or something equally silly."

Charles was relieved to return home to his flat that night. He had felt in his bones all day that at any time, the police would be knocking at his door. Now at home, he was more at ease. He had taken Jim's warning to heart, and had no intention of doing anything silly like splashing out or causing worry to his mother, or his employer Dan Jones, especially as he was now well on the way to reaching his ambition and becoming a heavy goods driver like his father. He thought it was high time he cut off his connection with his friends Jim and Peter, who had no doubt used him in their nefarious activities.

The following morning, Charles went to work and was pleased to find that he had to accompany one of the most experienced drivers to Dover Docks to pick up a valuable load. He was very happy, and felt that this at least confirmed his thoughts. He must make his way forward as a company driver.

He was a little taken aback when he found that he was travelling for quite a way along the road he had taken with the lorry load of 'snout'. He even felt like ducking down as they later passed the pub car park where he had dumped the lorry. To his relief, the vehicle was no longer there, and there was no evidence of police in the area. Ron, the driver, was not keen to let Charles take a turn at the wheel, and as they passed the pub car park again on the return journey, Charles was even pleased. Yet he found it almost impossible not to stare into the parking area to see if there were any police around, and felt sure that had he been driving, he might even have let his imagination or conscience take over, and ruin his concentration.

John Swain

Back at the yard, Dan Jones called Charles into his office. "How did you enjoy that ride today son?" he said. "You had a very valuable load on there today, and that is why you did not have a chance to drive. Just be patient, your turn will come. All you have to do is to keep your eyes open, and learn these routes. They are the ones you will be taking when you get your heavy goods licence, and it is as well to know the roads in advance. It is an advantage to me too. When I take on a driver, he has to learn these routes, and that takes up company time and money.

The following few weeks went on very much the same for Charles, with the usual visits to Tony's café for a chat with his mates. It soon became quite obvious that Jim did not have another job lined up. Quite wisely, he said that it would be better to leave lorries alone until the Paddock Wood job had blown over completely. In the meantime, he was looking into one or two things, and would be needing a driver soon.

According to Jim, what was needed was another 'run in slaughter' which they could drive a lorry into, and keep it behind a high fence, and locked gate or gates. This sounded like a good idea, but the rent would soon use up what cash they had between them.

"I'm working on it," said Jim, "and so is Peter. Leave it to us. We already have our eyes on a place at New Cross. If we can get hold of the bloke who owns it we should be in business again soon." Jim went on to explain that the place he had in mind was in Beckton Street, off Arlington Road, down New Cross way. "It backs on to a railway line, and the owner lives somewhere in the road, so it should be safe."

Quite by coincidence, the following day Charles was asked to make a delivery at Blackheath, so on his way back he toured round the area Jim had mentioned. Sure enough, there was a large long yard at one end of Beckton Street with two high gateways, and high corrugated iron fencing. A large lorry could be driven into one gate, and out of the other. Or it could be left in the yard, and there was no way it could be seen from the roadway. From a driver's point of view it was ideal for what Charles thought Jim had in mind. Whether or not it would suit both Jim and Peter was another thing, but he had no control over their thoughts. He reported his findings to Jim, who said he would look into the matter.

It was nearly a week before the trio met up again at Tony's. Peter had got hold of Fast Lou, he had made enquiries and found that the yard was rented by the Council to a man named Ted Best, who lived in Arlington Road and could probably see the yard in question from his first floor window. The trouble was, who was this Ted Best? Could he be approached and, more importantly, could he be trusted?

Jim decided that he was going to do just what the Law would do. He was going to sit up in the area, and keep 'obbo' on the yard. He wanted to see just what went on in the yard and locality, and to find out if the local coppers on the beat dropped in there for a cup of tea.

That would be the last straw! It was, however, one of the important points that had to be cleared up before taking any positive action. Furthermore, was there a lot of vehicle movement to and from the yard? It all had to be known before anything was done. And what about the local inhabitants? Did they take much notice of the goings on in the yard?

His detective work paid off. An elderly couple from Beckton Street were regular visitors to the public house at the end of Arlington Road, where it meets the Old Kent Road. They were pensioners who liked a pint, and welcomed Jim's offer to buy them a Guinness, and chat. They told Jim where they lived, and he mentioned that he thought it must be noisy there because of the trains. No, they had lived there for forty years, and had got used to it.

"But there's a great big yard right opposite your house. Doesn't that get noisy at times?"

"Not Really," was the reply. "Mr Best sometimes does a few car repairs in there, but it is pretty quiet generally."

Jim left his new-found friends after a brief chat. They were a very pleasant couple, and he did not want to force the issue with them. He decided to return the following day with Peter, and then perhaps approach Ted Best to tune up the Beetle.

They arrived at 8am and all was quiet. Just after nine o'clock, a man aged about sixty walked into Beckton Street and opened up the padlocked gates of the yard. Surely this had to be the man Ted Best. It was.

Peter got out of the car and walked into the yard. He walked over to the man who had just entered, and asked if he worked on Volkswagon motors.

"What's the trouble?" the man asked.

"Well, not much, but I have only just bought it, it sounds a bit rough, and I think it needs a tune up," said Peter.

"Bring it in, and I'll see what I can do."

Peter explained that the car was in the street outside, and that he had a mate with him. He then drove the car into the yard. Peter and Jim then sat on a bench in the yard chatting, whilst the work was done on the V.W.

Whoever this character was, he certainly knew his way

round an engine. After about half an hour, he turned to Peter and said, "That sounds better, doesn't it?" On being asked how much, he wanted for the work, he said, "Will three quid be O.K?" Peter gave him five pounds, and indicated that if he cared to meet them in the pub at the end of Arlington Road at lunchtime, he would buy him a pint because he was pleased with the way he had done the job. The man agreed, they shook hands and parted.

Opposite the public house in Arlington Road was a second hand car lot. "Stay in the car Jim," said Peter, "that car lot is owned by a Jewish fellow, and I think I know him. I'm going over to have a 'bunny' with him."

After about twenty minutes, Peter returned to the car. He told Jim that the man who had done the job was undoubtedly Ted Best. He had no 'form', but was a bit of a wheeler dealer in cars. He was a straight man to deal with, and didn't ask silly questions. Peter felt that with the right approach, they might well have found the 'slaughter' they were looking for.

They both then drove off for a tour of the locality, primarily to ascertain whether there were any likely obstacles to bringing strange vehicles into the area. Nothing was found that caused them any adverse thought. At 12.30, they both returned to the public house in Arlington Road. The man from the yard was at the counter in the Saloon Bar, and insisted on buying the lads a drink. Peter introduced himself and Jim. The man then introduced himself as Ted Best, saying, "Everyone round here knows me."

A conversation between the three men went on until just after two o'clock. By this time Mr Best, had agreed to buy from Peter any 'half straight' car he cared to bring in. This was a very satisfactory meeting, but it had to be properly sounded out before any action was taken. Peter had made his mind up how he would deal with this.

The next stop was at a car dealer in Tooting. Peter knew the owner, and said that he wanted to borrow the Ford Prefect on the front, and would be back either with it, or the cash, £200, that evening. There was no problem, and he drove it out of the compound.

Peter drove the car to their yard in Back Church Lane, and when Jim arrived he drove it into the arch. The following morning, Peter drove the Ford Prefect over to Ted Best's yard. "This one belongs to a couple who are away on holiday and will not be back for a fortnight. We have no log book, but there is no worry. It won't be missed or get circulated until they return and find the bloody thing missing. It's got to be worth a hundred quid. What do you think Ted?"

Ted Best was delighted. He slapped Peter's hand and said, "Done! When do you want paying?"

"I'll leave that to you," said Peter. "As soon as you like, I'm not rushing you, understand?"

"That's all right," said Ted. "Give me a few days, then come and see me again." Peter shook his hand, said, "I'll be back" and left.

Peter later looked in at Tony's café, and met Jim. He told him what he had done. Jim was not at all pleased. "Jeez!" he said. "You go out and do a tun in cold blood. What do you expect me to say?"

"Take it easy," said Peter. "I know my business, we have to sound out this character first. If he's OK to be one of us we will get our run in slaughter for a tun. If he's not, The law will be pulling me in for running a stolen car into him, and what a bloody shock they will get!"

The following morning, Peter returned to Tooting, and

with many apologies to his friend for taking so long with the deal, handed over £200. There was no hard feeling, and his friend was delighted, for at least his book would show that he had made another sale. What he did not know was that Peter still had the log book, which he would use when the time was right.

As far as Peter was concerned, this was the way to do business. Genuine legal business. He had made an investment, and everything hinged on his reception when he returned to Ted Best later in the week.

The time duly came when he made his way down the Old Kent Road, and stopped outside Ted's yard. "Come into the office," said Ted. Peter did not expect this, but at the dead end of one of Ted's railway arches, he had built himself something of an office with a table and some chairs, together with a metal filing cabinet. What a surprise! Sitting down on his desk such as it was, Ted opened a drawer, and pulled out an envelope. He tossed this across to Peter. "There's £120 there, any more cars like that, don't hesitate, just drive them in."

Peter expressed his appreciation for the extra cash. He had only asked for £100. This man was a good man to deal with, and there had been no reception committee from the local constabulary to meet him, which meant a lot. Sitting opposite Ted, Peter started talking about real money. He told Ted that he did occasionally come across some lorry loads of good saleable gear. The trouble was, he also needed somewhere safe to leave it whilst it was split up and sold. How did Ted feel about assisting in this business?

There had been a time during this discussion when Ted did not seem to grasp the situation. At the end of the talk, however, there was no doubt he had taken in everything that had been said. He stood up, reached his hand over the table, and said, "I am sure we can assist each other, providing we act sensibly." Peter pointed out that there were three people involved, and that Ted made the fourth. The profits were split equally four ways.

Finally, Peter pointed out that he would, however need to bring one of the others down so that he could work out how best to be able to use his yard, bearing in mind that some fairly large lorries would be brought in. They would if possible drive in one entrance, and out of the other. Also as the yard consisted of three railway arches, one would have to be used as a store.

Ted Best could see no problem, except that it would mean the place would have to be tidied up considerably.

"Leave that to me," said Peter. With that he turned to Ted, and said "Three of us will be down here Saturday morning at about eight o'clock, and we will sort this yard out over the weekend." He then got into his van and drove off.

CHAPTER 3
CHARLES SEES THE LIGHT

Charles was unable to take the Saturday morning off work. Mr Jones had an important delivery to be made, so he would not even ask to be excused. He did, however, go to the Arch at 7.30 the following morning, and there he explained to his friends that he could not be with them until after two in the afternoon. He would come later in the evening, and stay with them until it was too dark to work, if necessary. He then bade his friends goodbye, and made his way to his company yard in Cannon Street Road. The delivery on this occasion was to Letchworth, in Hertfordshire, and he had a fair idea of the best way to get there: travel due north out of London and over to the Edgware Road, then keep going north.

As he drove north, he realised that he would never be back to Cannon Street Road by two o'clock, and it would therefore be late evening before he could meet up with his mates at New Cross. There was nothing he could do about it, however, so he got on with his work. It was 2.30 before he managed to return to his company yard. To his surprise, Dan Jones was sitting in his office waiting for him. He was so pleased that Charles had taken the trouble and extra time needed to do the job, using up so much of his normal half day off. Patting him on the back, Dan invited Charles to take a seat, and announced that he would give him a £2 a week rise, and hoped that he would carry on working as he was. This was very pleasing indeed, and as Charles left the office and made his way towards New Cross, he found himself wondering whether or not he should completely part company with Jim and Peter. His boss was being so good to him.

Sitting down and talking to the boss in his office, something that no person had to his knowledge ever been allowed or invited to do in the past, made Charles feel very proud. He then realised that he had been there for nearly an hour. It was just after four o'clock before Charles made the yard in Beckton Street. Jim and Peter were working away, and with the aid of some timber he had brought in that morning, Peter had completed his framework for the arch, and cleared out all the rubbish which was piled up in the yard.

They complained that he had been a long while, but in the face of Charles' apology, did not make an issue of it. In fact, Jim finally said that it was as well Charles had done the work, for if ever there was a question about him, he was at least in full time and regular employment.

It was agreed that they would all go over to Limehouse and try and find Peter's friend Fred Stone, and perhaps have a curry. The object of looking for Fred Stone was that he was always looking out for drivers with valuable loads. He had taken advantage of the fact that many lorries carrying such loads from the north of the country travelled through Limehouse to ports on the South Coast. They therefore used Rotherhithe or Blackwall Tunnel, close to Limehouse. Fred had made a habit of befriending such drivers, and taking them for an Indian or Chinese meal in Limehouse, and had become accepted by these travellers as a useful contact in the area. Some of these friendships that had grown to the extent that on occasions, he had travelled with them to the port, or been brought back to London by them when the load had been delivered .

All agreed that a curry would be a change from Tony's pie and chips. They then made their way to a small and almost insignificant Indian café that was called, of all things 'Hell's Kitchen.' This was in West India Dock Road, almost opposite Limehouse Police Station.

According to Jim this had to be a joke. There was nobody in the ground floor part of this so-called restaurant. It was no bigger than a long narrow passageway, extending to the rear of the building. Tables were set out in line, and at least the area was spotlessly clean, but there was no sign of anyone serving. To the left of this narrow area there was a flight of stairs leading downwards. "Don't worry," said Peter. He then shouted out "Where are you Simon?"

A voice with an Indian accent echoed up from below, "Down here. Is that you Peter?"

The only thing appetising about this place was the smell - if you liked curry, and these lads did like it. They were hungry already, and the tang of the curry certainly tickled the taste buds.

Peter led the way below. Here there was a similar layout as on the ground floor, but with one very obvious difference. In an alcove, to the right of the end of the stairway, sat   a very stout Indian stirring away at a large cauldron that was heated by a gas ring underneath it. The contents were simmering away, and the smell of the curry was wonderful.

Peter introduced his friends. "This is Simon Gabohan," he said, "he comes from Trincomalee, and makes the best curry in London. Lords and ladies come here, so don't

worry about the size of the place, and the lack of wait-
ers. He does the lot, he cooks, serves, and takes the
money."

They ordered three curries and Charles and Jim looked
on with interest as Simon, using the very long ladle that
he had been stirring the mixture with, scooped out of the
cauldron three helpings of his famous curry onto steam-
ing beds of rice. As Peter accepted his helping, he said
to Simon, "Has Fred Stone been in lately?"

"No," said Simon, "but he always comes in on Saturday night, he should be in here soon."

The trio set about their curries with gusto, and each
agreed that it was the best they had ever tasted. Then, to
the surprise of Charles and Jim, Simon asked if they
wanted some more. "You will have to have some more,"
said Peter, "if you refuse his offer, he would take it as an
insult." So the plates were topped up by the host.

At a quarter past ten that night, Fred Stone arrived.
He was pleased to see Peter, and was introduced to his
two friends. He likewise had a curry from Simon's cauldron, and sat with them chatting away. Peter then paid
for all the meals, and told Fred that they needed some
timber for a job they were doing, and mentioned that he
wanted some lengths of four by two, and also some
planking. Fred said that he had plenty of wood that size,
and asked where he wanted it delivered. Peter gave him
the address of the yard in New Cross, and said that they
would all be there from nine o'clock the following morning. If Fred could bring the wood over in the morning,
Peter would pay on delivery. "I'll be there between nine
and ten in the morning with a load, and you can take
what you need," said Fred.

It was nearing midnight when the group parted company. The trio drove off to Back Church Lane, after bidding Simon and Fred Stone goodbye. On the journey, they all praised Simon's curry. "I thought you would enjoy it," said Peter. "But there is one thing you ought to know." He then went on to explain that Simon came from Trincomalee, in Ceylon, and had been a ship's cook just after the 1914-18 war, and had travelled the world on one particular ship. He was very happy until a new Captain of a different caste to Simon was brought in. This man made life very difficult for him.

Simon could do nothing about it, so as he had many friends in England, the next time the ship docked in the Pool of London, he jumped ship. At first, he worked in an Indian restaurant in Limehouse, but it was not long before he decided to go it alone, and rented that little place in Limehouse. His curry became very popular, and it was generally believed that since then, he had never cleaned out that big pot - he just added to it! Some people said it should not be allowed, but according to Simon, he only cooked chicken curry, and as the stove never went out, nothing could go off. Therefore there was nothing to worry about. I wonder?

Charles could hardly believe this, but as he had thoroughly enjoyed his meal, he decided to say nothing, and wait to see how his stomach behaved the following day. At Back Church Lane, they parted company, and Charles went back to his flat in Myrdle Street. He was glad he had warned his mother that he would be late home, and had a key to get in with. All was quiet when he entered, so he made his way to bed and slept soundly.

The following morning Charles met this colleagues, and drove with them to New Cross. Fred Stone was as good as his word, and arrived in Beckton Street, at 9.15.

John Swain

He had a nice load of old timber on the back of his lorry, and Peter selected what he needed and handed each piece down to Jim or Charles to take into the yard. When Peter had all that he required, and probably a little more, he asked Fred how much he owed him. "Twenty quid," said Fred.

"Done," said Peter and handed the amount over. They shook hands as Fred Stone drove off.

With the wood now in his possession, Peter set about making a pair of doors for the arch, and filling in around them. By the end of the afternoon, the arch was well secured and looked passable. The timber they had purchased was second hand, but quite good enough for its purpose. The day was rounded off by a quiet drink at the pub at the end of Arlington Road.

The main theme that Jim took up was the fact that now they had an excellent 'slaughter,' they had better find some 'work.' They would have to pay Ted Best something soon, and that meant they would have to go out and find some work. "I'll go and find another Ford Prefect," said Peter. "I know where there is one that is not used very much, and won't be missed for a few days."

Charles drove the van towards their base in Back Church Lane, but Peter had other ideas. He directed Charles to drive over to Lordship Lane, Dulwich.. There he told him to stop the van. He got out, and said, "When you see me drive a Ford Prefect out of that road," which he indicated, "take Jim back to Aldgate, and leave the van at the slaughter."

Shortly after Peter left, they saw a black Ford Prefect emerge from the road indicated, and sure enough, it was being driven by Peter. He gave them a wave and a thumbs up sign as he drove away. Charles did as he had been asked, and after dropping Jim off at Gardiners Corner, returned the van to their yard.

Peter made for Beckton Street, and after unlocking the main gates drove in. He put the Ford Prefect in the recently secured arch, closed up and left. He then went over to Ted Best's flat in Arlington Road, and told him what he had done. At the same time, he told Ted to sell it for what he could get, and they would split the profit in the way they had agreed. Ted was delighted, and said he thought he would be able to 'knock it out' within a day or so, with no worry at all.

That evening at Tony's café, Jim announced that he had a nice lorryload in mind, but that it would need a lot of work. He had been looking at a car park, used also by the occasional lorry in Greenwich. The result was that he was beginning to know the type of loads that were passing through the area, and laying up whilst the drivers went for a meal or refreshment.

The next few days had Charles acting as driver's mate to one of the company heavy lorry drivers, and travelling as far off as Birmingham. He was happy on two points. The curry had not upset him, so perhaps the story about Simon never cleaning out his big pot was a joke. He felt good. He also had plenty of opportunity to drive the lorry. In fact, when he drove the vehicle, Jack the driver watched over him, and commented on his driving as if he was an examiner. This was most useful, for Charles realised that he was beginning to get into the sort of bad habits in his driving that examiners look upon as a fault. Perhaps he had been a little over confident, but he felt sure that he was now making good progress with his driving.

On their return from Birmingham, Dan Jones sent for

Charles. They were going to need another heavy goods driver, and he had decided to arrange for a driving inspector to come in and examine Charles with a view to getting him the necessary HGV licence. He would therefore take Jack out as his mate the next day, and pick up a load from Reading. Then, subject to Jack's report, Dan would take the necessary action to get Charles through the last stage towards his licence.

Charles was at the yard early the following morning, and quite excited at the prospect of going out on what could be a real test of his ability. The drive out of the yard was the first part of this journey that made him think. The heavy Leyland lorry needed some coaxing out of the enclosed space where it had been parked, but he managed it without too much difficulty. At Jack's direction, he drove through the heavy traffic of the City of London. They then continued due west through Hammersmith, to the Great West Road, and on to a large depot at Reading. Pulling into the loading bay was the only part of the manoeuvring inside the yard that Charles found difficult. Jack, however, said that he had done well.

Their return journey was quite uneventful. They returned to the company yard without incident, and on arrival Jack stated that he was what he referred to as 'safe hands'. He also indicated that he would have no problem with the examiner, but would have to learn the route he was going to take before they went out. Dan Jones would tell him where he was to go on the day. It would be a normal company pick-up or delivery, but with the examiner, not a company driver.

Nothing further on the subject was said for a few days, and Charles worked for the most part as the van driver. On the Friday, however, when he arrived at the yard,

Dan Jones wanted to see him. He went to his office, and found a rather military looking man sitting opposite his boss. Mr Jones opened up the conversation by saying, "This is Mr Pearson. He is going to accompany you to Reading today, and I want you to take the Leyland, and collect some freight then bring it back here."

He then handed Charles the paperwork, and left the office. After collecting the keys of the Leyland from the Dispatch Office, Charles walked over to the Leyland. Mr Pearson was there, and clearly he was inspecting the vehicle: looking under it, kicking the tyres, and checking over the doors to see if they locked. He was a lot older than Charles, and gave the impression of being quite a fierce individual. Charles unlocked the cab door, and got into the driver's seat. "Shall we go now?" he asked.

Pearson climbed into the passenger seat, and said, "Right, where are we going?"

"Reading, Sir," said Charles, and with that he started the engine of the vehicle. Not wishing to take a different route to that which he had taken with Jack on the previous occasion, he drove on to the Great West Road once again. Mr Pearson said nothing, but he was clearly watching every move that Charles made. On arrival at the Reading Depot, he made his way to the loading bay, and got out of the cab. Still Mr Pearson said nothing.

After signing for the load, Charles got back into the cab, and was pleased that he had been in this yard before. He managed to drive out without any difficulty at all. The return journey was equally uneventful, and when he finally drove back into the Cannon Street Road, yard, he was beginning to wonder just what Mr Pearson would have to say. The examiner said nothing, however; he just got out of the cab, and strode across the yard to Dan

Jones' office. "The Governor wants you," said the Dispatch Clerk when Charles handed in his paper work.

Charles made his way to Dan Jones' office. Mr Pearson was sitting in the same chair that he had occupied in the morning, but this time he got up, walked over to Charles, and shook his hand. "Congratulations young man," he said. "You did everything that you should do during the journey there and back . Quite frankly, I have not felt so safe with a strange driver for a long while." Then, turning to Mr Jones, he said, "You can count yourself lucky Dan, he's a bloody good driver, one to be proud of." He then turned and left the office.

"That's it," said Mr Jones, as Pearson closed the door behind himself. "Now you have your licence, you will be paid full driver's rate plus whatever necessary, and accountable overtime that you incur. Congratulations lad, you've done well. Your father would have been very proud of you."

CHAPTER 4
A LORRY LOAD OF TINNED MEAT.

Charles walked home with a spring in his step. He had obtained what he had striven so hard for, and was now a fully paid, respected heavy goods driver like his father. How he wished that his father was still alive! He was so proud. When he told his mother the result of the day's outing, she did what many mothers do in similar circumstances - she burst into tears and hugged her son.

That evening, Charles made his way to Tony's café, and met Jim and Peter. He told them what had happened, and that he now had a licence to drive heavy goods vehicles. They both congratulated him warmly, but Charles felt a little guilty. They had both been so good to him. Now he would have to tell them that he could no longer be relied upon to turn out to assist them on so many jobs. His new job must come first, Van Dragging was not for him.

Peter looked very downhearted and said nothing. Jim, however, smiled broadly, and said ,"Of course you must look after your job, but that does not mean that we cannot still be friends just because your are not a Van Dragger, does it?"

Charles was relieved. "If I can help at any time, give me a shout," he said, "but I will not be able to turn out as much as I have before. I am so glad you understand."

The evening continued in a very subdued manner.

John Swain

There was no discussion about the New Cross Slaughter, or the big job that Jim had previously said he had in mind. Quite frankly, Charles was glad, because he did not want to turn down a request to help them out so soon.

It was at this point that Mary Morris walked into the café. She had been at school at the same time as Jim and Charles, and Charles had always fancied her. He invited her to sit with them and bought her a coffee and a bun. She was clearly pleased at the invitation, and entered into the small talk. Then at eleven o'clock, Charles walked her home.

The following morning, Charles reported to his firm in Cannon Street Road. There was a job waiting for him in the Dispatch Office, and he checked over the paper-work. He had been allocated Jack's Leyland lorry, and was directed to attend premises in Swindon, and bring the load back to the Cannon Street Road Yard. He there-fore made his way westward, after checking the route on his map.

He now had a strange feeling of power and owner-ship. This was his lorry, the one that he was responsible for. The cab was clean and comfortable, though there were a few creature comforts he would have to install. These were simple matters, such as making absolutely sure that he had Jack's old seat at his personal level and height. The glove compartment was handy, but he would have to fix a box or something between the two front seats where he could put his sandwiches and maps. Taken all round, he felt very comfortable and relaxed as he drove on.

He did not think about his mates, but down in Back Church Lane, Jim and Peter were having a quiet time. Peter was upset about Charles, and the fact that he now

48

had a regular job, and would not be able to help them out. Jim, on the other hand, accepted the situation without difficulty. "I am not in the slightest bit surprised," he said. "I always remember when I first got hold of him to come out on the 'hoist' in Boltons, years ago. It just was not in him to steal. He is, I am afraid, basically honest, and I am even surprised that we managed to get him to do some of the things he has done for us. That first jump up he did in Tooley Street, for example. He truly believed that the vehicle belonged to you."

But Peter's main worry was that Charles could now even 'grass' on them if he was ever questioned about his friendship and association with them. Jim, however, would not have this; he was quite convinced that Charles would never let them down. As far as he was concerned, Charles was still his friend, and he trusted him implicitly.

"What about that bird Mary?" said Peter. "You know she's a Coppers daughter?"

Jim explained that he knew that because she was at school at the same time as he was with Charles, and Charles was always keen on her, even then.

It was finally agreed that they would have to look round for another man to assist them, and preferably someone who could drive well, and drive a lorry, because they were going into the 'jump up' business, big-time! With that Jim suggested that they take the van out, and made their way to Greenwich where there was a large parking area where lorries sometimes parked either overnight, or whilst the driver had a meal in town.

As they arrived at the parking area, a large Denis Lorry drove in. "That's a bit of luck," said Jim. "It looks like a heavy load." They watched the driver as he locked up his cab and climbed down. He then walked away from

John Swain

the vehicle park, and entered the nearby Admiral Hardy public house. Jim, and Peter followed. There he walked up to the counter and ordered a pint of beer and a sandwich. Our two characters stood beside the driver, who was known in the pub as George, and struck up a conversation with him. He had driven from Folkestone, and was on his way to his company premises at Dagenham.

This was his usual run, once a week run, and always on a Thursday. He usually came into the Hardy because they made 'bloody good sandwiches', and Greenwich is so handy for the Blackwall Tunnel, and on to Dagenham.

"What about your lorry?" said Jim. "There's nowhere to park a big one round here."

"There's not supposed to be," said George, "but I park up near the Cutty Sark. I am only there for an hour, and by the time they have found a copper, I am back and away. I never leave it for more than an hour."

True to his word, George left the Admiral Hardy when his hour was almost up. Peter then left, indicating that he would be back in a few minutes. He followed George at a distance, and noted the index number of the lorry, which George started up and drove off immediately. Returning to the public house, he told Jim what he had seen, and said that next week they would be in the same bar from about 1pm.

There had been no indication as to what was on the Denis lorry, but both felt that it had been well loaded. Furthermore, they agreed that it was only a matter of time spent watching George, if he came regularly, before they would get to the bottom of the business his company was in. There was also the worry about getting a driver, now that it seemed they would be without Charles. Peter was satisfied that he could 'hot wire' the Denis, but would not want to drive it

The next stop was Warrington Road, Walworth. Jim knew a man there who had a greengrocery stall, and he had a small lorry which he used to go to Covent Garden market to get his supplies, and also those for other people in the area. Bert Hinchcliffe was a man who had made good in the area. He was well respected for not overcharging his business customers. He was even called upon by the stall holders in East Street Market at times to get supplies for them, on a 'no questions asked' basis. He was not exactly an angel, he had in fact served nine months in prison for G.B.H, and had avoided capture by the police in relation to his many nefarious deals.

Jim strolled up to Bert at his stall, and told him that they had a lorry load that was nearing the 'ready eyed' stage. In a week or maybe two, they should be able to take it providing Bert could drive a fairly big Denis lorry.

"No problem," said Bert, "providing I have not got to drive it too far, and you can hot wire it."

He was told that he would only have to drive it for about three or four miles, but they would want to be able to get hold of him early on the day when they would take it. That suited Bert, because he lived in the road, and could always get his wife to look after the stall if he had to leave it.

The next stop that day was at Beckton Street. Ted Best was working on a taxi, and the driver was standing by. He indicated to Jim that he should come back the next day, and he would have his motor ready. Jim said, "OK, be here at about midday", then turned and they both left.

"He's a shrewd one," said Peter. "It's nice to have an unannounced reception like that dealt with in such a way.

You can't always trust cabbies. At least we know we can trust the bold Ted Best now."

The following Thursday morning, Jim and Peter met at Back Church Lane. "Let's pick up Bert Hinchcliffe this morning," said Jim, "then take him over to Greenwich, but first we will go over and see Ted Best and see what he has to say."

They got into the van, and drove over to Beckton Street. Ted was pleased to see them, and went into his office, returning with an envelope which he gave to Jim. "There's 120 quid there," he said. "I like Ford Prefects, they are usually easy ones to knock out, just needed a tune up and general tidy up internally." Ted then went on to apologise for sending them away the previous day, but Jim assured him that he had done the right thing, and that they fully understood the situation.

Leaving New Cross, they made their way to Warrington Road, Walworth. Bert Hinchcliffe was not at his stall, but his wife was there, and said that he would only be a few minutes. They decided to wait, and after about ten minutes Bert returned, full of apologies for keeping them waiting. Jim told him that they wanted him to come with them to look at a vehicle they had their eyes on. Bert was all for this, and got into the back of the van.

They drove over to Greenwich, arriving there at a quarter to twelve. They found a parking place near the Cutty Sark, and sat and waited. George arrived in his Denis lorry just after half past twelve. He locked up his vehicle, and went straight over to the Admiral Hardy. Peter left Bert and Jim in the van, and went over to the Denis. He was more interested in getting into the lorry, which he managed without difficulty. He was only in the vehicle about two minutes.

He then got out of the vehicle, then went round to the rear of it and peered inside to see what it was carrying. Cases of tinned foodstuffs - very useful! He returned to the van and said, "I can fix the ignition in a couple of minutes, it's a piece of cake. How do you feel about it Bert?"

Bert was delighted. "If you can wire it up that quick, there is no trouble at all, just how long have we got before the balloon goes up?" Jim told him that was no problem, and said that he would show him exactly where he would have to drive the lorry, but on the day, all he had to do was to follow the van. Also that Jim and Peter would be in it and would guide him to the slaughter.

It was then explained to Bert that they would pick him up the following Thursday morning at about ten, and go over to Greenwich and wait for the arrival of George in his Denis lorry. Before leaving their parking place near the Cutty Sark, Jim decided that they should wait for George's return, to see if he had any obvious worry, particularly since Peter had been in his vehicle. Jim also thought it would be a good idea to follow him to see if he adopted the route he had previously suggested, going to the Blackwall Tunnel on his way back to Dagenham. This was agreed.

It was exactly half past one when George returned to his lorry. He unlocked his cab, got in, and drove off almost immediately. He turned in the parking area with some difficulty, because it was quite crowded with visitors' cars. From the parking area he turned left into the Greenwich one-way system, then left past the old naval college, and on to the turn-off to the Blackwall Tunnel, which he took immediately.

Jim slapped the steering wheel of the van, and said in a loud voice, "That settles that. We will have that one next Thursday." He then turned the van and made his way towards New Cross. Arriving at Arlington Road, Jim told Bert that was where he had to make for and, indicating the railway line, told him that they would guide him to the slaughter on the day. He then continued towards Warrington Road, and dropped Bert off at the end of the road.

The two lads drove back to their yard at Back Church Lane, and parked up the van. Jim took the envelope he had received from Ted Best in New Cross out of his pocket. He gave Peter £50, put 50 in his own pocket, and said to Peter, "I will give Charlie the odd 20 quid, you never know when we might need him."

The following morning, Jim and Peter met up at the yard, and decided to go down to the farm in Kent. "That has been a wonderful slaughter," said Jim. "You did bung that farmer Peter, didn't you? We never know when we might need him again." Peter assured him that he had done the right thing, and that a visit to the farmer would do no harm.

It was a lovely day, and it seemed ideal for the purpose. The Kent countryside was at its best, and it was not long before Jim pulled into the side of the road and purchased a bag of plums from one of the farm shops. "Better than Tony's buns!" said Peter. As they sat in the van enjoying a few of the plums, Peter said, "While we're on the subject of Tony, I think it will be as well to leave that café out from now on. I bet that Charlie of yours is knocking about with the Morris girl, whose father is a cozza, and the less we see of her the better."

The farmer was delighted to see Peter, and invited them both in for a drink. This rather surprised them, and not knowing what they were in for, they entered the farmhouse and sat down in a very spacious lounge. What a surprise! It was quite a palace, fitted out with all of the modern conveniences that were not usually equated with farmhouses.

"That was a nice one you had last time," said the farmer. "Got any more lined up like that?"

"We have one in mind," said Peter, "but I will let you know in advance, if I can."

The farmer shook his head, and invited them to come outside and have another look at the barn where they had put the last load. He had put some of his tools and equipment down one side of the barn, whilst the other side was completely clear.

"If you have a load to get rid of in a hurry," said the farmer, "just drive it down here, and straight in. You can tell me afterwards, if I don't see you arriving. You seem to know what you are doing, and you have been fair with me, so now you know the form." He then indicated a large folded tarpaulin by his equipment, and said, "That's the cover you had last time, I shall leave it there for you to use again if necessary."

They thanked him, and returned to the farm house with him. There, between them, they disposed of the best part of a bottle of Scotch before driving off.

Very little was said on the return journey to London, except, perhaps just one remark that in truth said it all. Jim, obviously pleased, and excited with the reception they had received, did what he so often did when in that frame of mind: he slapped the steering wheel with both hands and said, "What a gentleman, we are now really in business."

On arrival back at the yard, they shook hands and parted, agreeing to meet at the yard on Thursday morning, prior to picking up Bert Hinchcliffe.

The following evening, Jim decided to pay a short visit to Tony's café. He had not given Charles the £20 from the last Ford Escort deal. Charles was sitting at one of the tables with Mary Morris, chatting away. He was glad to see Jim, and they shook hands, but there was little said. Charles was more interested in talking to Mary, and Jim had noticed that Tony wanted to speak to him, apparently urgently.

He was able to slip Charles the £20 under the table, and immediately left the café. Tony followed him out into Cable Street. They stopped about 100 yards away from the café. Tony had missed Jim and Peter, but said that they had done the right thing by not coming to the café regularly. Mary's father was Detective Sergeant Jim Morris from Leman Street Police Station. He had graduated from being a uniformed Constable, and made the rank of Sergeant in the Criminal Investigation Department. In fact, he was a very busy 'cozza' in the area, and would soon put two and two together if the lads were seen too often in the same place. Also, he often met his daughter in Tony's café.

Tony was clearly worried, and felt that Jim Morris was getting to know too much about the customers in his café. As for Charles, he was very friendly with Mary, and with her father, and it was as well that they had split from him. With that they parted company.

The visit had been well worth while. Peter in particular had been worried about the fact that Charles obviously intended a closer association with Mary Morris, something that Jim, perhaps out of loyalty, had ignored. This, however, was proof positive of the dangers of being seen in regular company with Charles. Jim also felt that he owed a little more than just thanks to Tony for his very timely warning.

On the following Thursday morning, Jim and Peter met as agreed at the Back Church Lane yard. Jim told Peter what had happened on his visit to the café, and recounted Tony's very wise warning about using the café too often. Peter nodded sagely in full agreement.

Peter quietly said, "Well, I felt that as soon as I saw the two of them together. That Jim Morris has nicked a lot of people round here, we don't want him making enquiries about us."

They made their way over Tower Bridge, to Warrington Road. Bert was at his stall, and ready to accompany them to Greenwich. His wife took over the stall, and they drove off. On the way there, Jim told Bert that if the job came off, after they had unloaded the lorry, he would have to drive it over the other side of the Thames and leave it somewhere. Peter then suggested that he should drive it through Rotherhithe Tunnel, and leave it possibly in the Roman Road, Bow area. Then, when it was discovered, the police on the other side of the river would be busy working on it, a long way from either New Cross or Greenwich.

Arriving near the Cutty Sark, Jim parked the van and they remained inside, chatting away. At about 12.30, they watched as George parked up his Denis lorry about 100 yards away. Peter told Jim to follow George as he got out of the cab, and to make sure that he went to the Admiral Hardy public house. Then, turning to Bert he said, "I shall go over to the Denis and get in on the driver's side. Give me two or three minutes, then you come over and get in, also on the driver's side. Then, when I leave, you turn the vehicle and follow us in the van to New Cross."

"Got it," said Bert.

Peter left the van as George got out of the lorry. He then went over to the Denis and, lying down on the floor of the cab, tinkered with the under dashboard wiring, finally starting up the motor. At that moment, Bert climbed into the driver's seat. Then, indicating a small plug and socket, Peter said, "Leave this alone until you either want to or have to stop the engine. To stop the engine, pull the plug out, and put it in this glove, which I'll hang on the dashboard. When you want to start the engine again, put the plug into the socket, and press the starter button."

"Understood," said Bert.. Peter then got out of the cab, and went back to the van.

Bert had no difficulty in turning the lorry round, and once facing towards the Greenwich one-way system, the van turned and got in front of the lorry. Following the van was quite easy for Bert and it was only about a quarter of an hour before they were in Arlington Road. The van turned into Beckton Street, and found the first entry gates open. Stopping the van, Peter got out and directed Bert to drive into the yard and pull up by the end arch.

Ted Best acknowledged the new arrivals by giving a thumbs up signal from his bench. The trio - Peter, Jim and Bert - started to unload the lorry. They placed the contents, which consisted of tinned meat, bully beef, Spam, and the likes, into the end arch, which Peter had blanked off previously.

It took them a half hour to unload the Dennis, and stack the cases of tinned meat in the arch. It was quite surprising just how much room there was in those old railway arches, something that they were all very grateful for.

Turning to Bert, Peter said, "Old George has about now finished up his pint and sandwich in the Admiral Hardy. He will now walk back round to the Cutty Sark car park, to his lorry. He will find it hard to believe that it has been stolen. That's another quarter of an hour on our side. He will then go round to the local Police Station, which will take him more time. Then after the Police have taken his particulars, and notified his company, we still have time to spare. It will be an hour before the lorry gets circulated as stolen. So Bert my friend, get that lorry out of here, and over the other side of the river as fast as you can, but don't get done for speeding."

Bert laughed aloud, and said, "Don't worry, I'm off." As he got back into the cab, Peter went over to him, and said, "When you have decided where you are going to leave it, switch off, reach up one of the wires as far as you can, and give the wire a sharp tug. Put the plug and socket in your pocket. We will need them again for a future occasion."

Bert drove the lorry out of the yard without difficulty, and was soon away up Arlington Road, making for Rotherhithe Tunnel. Once through the tunnel, he turned right at Commercial Road East, and carried on until he came to Burdett Road. He turned into Burdett Road, and continued northwards crossing Bow Road, into Grove Road, then on to Roman Road. He continued along Roman Road until he came to Hewlett Road, where he turned in and parked just round the corner from Roman Road. After wiping the steering wheel, and anything else he may have touched, then putting the plug, sock and glove in his pocket, he tugged one of the wires loose, got down from the cab, and walked off.

It was only about half past two, and a fine afternoon. There were quite a few people around, undoubtedly many of them making their way to Roman Road market, but nobody took any notice of Bert. He therefore continued on his way feeling quite relaxed. There was a strong temptation to look back, but he was too old in the tooth for that. He just wanted to get back to his stall at Warrington Road, Walworth.

It was nearly an hour before he arrived back on his home ground. His wife was serving at the stall, and business seemed to be running smoothly. He felt extremely satisfied with his day's work, and immediately did the rounds to see where he could 'place' some of the recent acquisition. He knew most of the dealers in the area who would welcome a chance to invest in a couple of dozen cases of tinned meat at the right price.

At half past five, Jim and Peter arrived at the stall. Mrs Hinchliffe was serving a customer, and on seeing them shouted over, "He will be about ten minutes, better hang around, I think he will want to see you." They acknowledged her call with a wave, and sat on a low wall nearby. Bert returned in about a quarter of an hour. He was happy in the knowledge that he had probably sold half of the load in the slaughter to local people in four lots, with 'cash on the nail'. This sounded all very well but Peter, being cautious, wanted to know if Bert could trust these people.

Bert hastened to assure both Peter and Jim that he had long been buying and selling anything that was going in the area to these people, and there had never been any trouble. He then handed the plug and socket to Peter, and said, "A very useful piece of kit to be sure, Peter. Thank you."

Peter did not share Bert's enthusiasm for selling some of the recent haul locally, and warned him to be cautious. He also advised him that a little loose talk could

The Van Draggers

bring unwanted local interest. He warned that the Police
are usually watching out for any new line in cheap goods
that suddenly appears in markets. "Don't forget Bert,"
said Peter, "Carter Street Nick is only a few minutes' walk
from Warrington Road and East Street market, so please
be careful. There are plenty of young cozzers about, trying to make a name for themselves, and they listen to
anything and everything. In any event, we don't deliver
to market stalls."

The discussion continued with Jim pointing out that
his policy was only to deliver to proven safe lock-ups,
when there is nobody around. Always to people who
could be trusted not to talk openly about their deals. He
also pointed out that the cases containing the tins would
have to be destroyed, preferably burnt, because they were
identifiable. Something that must be pointed out to the
customer at the outset, although if that person was any
good, he would realise that point when he clinched the
deal.

"I might have a better way," said Bert. "I will find the
punters, and when I know how many they want, I will
collect the cases from the Slaughter and deliver them my-
self. These people know me, I've been helping them out
for years." Peter and Jim were still not happy, but if that
was how Bert wanted it, he would have to realise that he
was on his own. His share was a quarter of the take, and
if he got arrested whilst hawking the goods, he could
only blame himself. Even in the face of this fact, he had
undoubtedly made up his mind on the subject, but he
promised to be ultra careful.

It was finally agreed that the following midday, Peter
and Jim would meet at the Warrington Arms public house,
and have a final discussion. Before parting, however,
Peter pointed out that they only wanted to make four

deliveries. They did not want to bring attention to the slaughter by too many comings and goings. Also, whoever wanted to purchase goods should take one van load, not just a few cases. It was better that the buyers did the split deliveries, not Bert.

Before parting, Peter said, "I know a man over in the Shepherds Bush area who might even take the lot, so I think I'll go and see him tonight. I should be able to know the position and tell you something positive, one way or another, tomorrow."

As Jim and Peter drove along the Walworth Road, Peter said, "Why not go over there now? I think I know where to find Wally Fish, and he is quite a buyer for the Shepherds Bush market."

"Sounds like a good idea," said Jim.

At the Elephant and Castle intersection, they turned left along Newington Butts, then turned right towards Vauxhall Bridge. Once over the bridge, they turned left along Grosvenor Road, continuing way past Earls Court to Shepherds Bush Green. Here they turned left and made their way to Goldhawk Road. They parked the van in Wingate Road, close to the Royal Oak public house, then walked into the Saloon Bar. As they entered the bar a loud voice called out, "What are you doing this far over, Peter?"

With that Peter introduced Jim to Wally Fish, explaining that he might be in business for some tinned meat in the next few days, and wanted to know if Wally was interested. Wally replied that he was loaded up at the moment with tinned goods, and did not want to take on another delivery. He suggested that if he could have a week, perhaps he could accommodate Peter's goods then.

Peter told him that he would make contact with him

again in a week. He then went on to ask Wally just what sort of goods he was interested in. "Any bloody thing," replied Wally. "Just look at the load and ask yourself whether it could be sold in the market place, and try me again."

Between them, they had a good drink. Wally was clearly very pleased to see Peter, and his mate and continued to impress on them that he would buy most things by the load. Unfortunately, at the moment his store was full up, but if Peter came back in a week, he was sure he could help him.

At closing time our two men left the public house, and started back in the direction of their home area. Between them they were happy with the contact and the fact that they had a buyer for loads, even the tinned meat in a week, if they were unable to shift it. Also, it would do no harm to leave the meat for at least a week. It was safe where it was now stored, in the railway arch.

During the period now under review, Charles was thoroughly enjoying his work as a company heavy goods driver. He travelled far and wide on company business, and his work was well appreciated by Dan Jones the boss. He was thankful that he'd had the good sense to part from his friends Jim and Peter, because he felt that sooner or later they would both be caught in the act of stealing something. His loyalty now was firstly to his mother, his dead father, and the company that his father used to work for, which now employed him.

But there was more to it than that. Charles was very fond of Mary Morris, and although her father had been asking Tony questions about him, Charles felt that he would like to speak with him and let him know his feelings for his daughter. On his next meeting with Mary, he told her that he would like to talk to her father about the two of them. Mary did not think that would help much. Charles nevertheless persisted, and said he wanted to talk to him and put his mind at rest, because he was now in no way connected with his friend Jim's activities.

The morning after their meeting with Wally Fish, Jim and Peter met at their yard and, after a short discussion, made their way over to the Warrington Arms public house. Bert was already there, and full of what he felt was good news. He had one man who would take half of the load, and two others who would take the rest. All cash on delivery. Furthermore, they would be waiting to hear from him at their yard at seven o'clock that evening.

Bert was quite convinced that he knew the people concerned extremely well and had known them for many years. It was agreed that he should come to New Cross with his van, and meet them in Beckton Street at six o'clock. An agreement was reached, and they parted company. Jim and Peter made their way to the local café for a late lunch, and then drove over to New Cross.

Ted Best was there, working on a Ford Prefect. "You love those motors," said Peter.

"They are the easiest to work on and sell, what more can I ask?" said Ted. "What are you doing here, anyway?"

"A good point," replied Peter. "We hope to empty that arch this evening, and be able to give you some wages before the day is out."

Ted rubbed his hands together, saying, "Carry on, the wife will be pleased." They then opened up the arch, and backed the van into the doorway and commenced loading up the cases of tinned meat. It was quite surprising how much the van would take, for it was obvious that the load on board would be a quarter of what was in the arch.

Bert Hinchcliffe arrived in Beckton Street at 6pm, and was ushered into the yard with his van. He was loaded up with the same amount as Jim and Peter had placed in their vehicle. They then sat down for a smoke and a chat. "These two loads will go into a run-in on Brandon Street," said Bert. "Then one will have to be taken to Browning Street and the last one to Neate Street. Now, if you will follow me I will guide you to the Brandon Street drop. I will only need Jim to come with me. I suggest that Peter, you stay behind to lock up and let us in when we return."

Jim followed Bert in his van, and on arrival at a yard in Brandon Street that was open, Bert drove in and waved Jim to also enter. As soon as he stopped, two men came to the van and unloaded it, stacking the cases inside a large shed. When both vans had been unloaded, Bert and one of the men went to a corner of the shed, and entered into a close conversation. Finally, Jim saw Bert being handed a large envelope, which he put into his inside pocket. Bert then called out, "See you at the other end, Jim", got into his van and drove out of the yard.

When Jim got to Beckton Street, Bert was already in the yard and loading up his van. "I will put the remainder on my van," said Jim.

"No point," said Bert. I will drop this lot and come back for the rest. These people know me and it is best that I go alone." He then handed Jim the envelope he had received in Brandon Street, and said, "While I am away, you can work this lot out, and I will have my whack when we settle up after the last load." He then got into his van and drove off.

"What do you think of that, Peter?" said Jim. "He's a cool one, and I am sure that he knows his business."

"Seems OK to me," replied Peter, "but I will only rest easy after we have got rid of the lot."

They had hardly finished chatting about Bert's ability to get rid of his load, when he returned. Peter opened up the gates of the yard, and he drove in. Before he loaded up, Bert produced from an inside pocket a huge roll of banknotes, and said, "That's for the last load.

The following few weeks were spent in something best referred to as a state of limbo. Both Jim and Peter were doing what people in their style of occupation would call, 'giving their eyes a treat'. There were plenty of 'tiddlers' - small vans with small loads and small profits - to be had. Such jobs, however, had the same amount of risk as going for a big one. Thus, both Jim and Peter decided that if they were to take on a job, it had to be worthwhile. They also decided to continue watching points and to settle only for sizeable and profitable loads of easily saleable goods.

CHAPTER 5
BISCUITS GALORE, AND THE NEAR MISS.

It was exactly three weeks before such a load presented itself. The information was that lorry loads of biscuits were regularly transported from a factory in the Midlands to Southampton. The agent for the people concerned had an office in Jamaica Road, just over Tower Bridge. The driver usually arrived near the agent's office between eight and nine in the morning, and then paid a visit to the office. There was no information as to what he went to the agents office for, but it was felt that it was most likely to be for clearance documents - a feeling prompted by the ultimate delivery point, Southampton, and perhaps connected with the delivery or even the shipping of the load.

Whilst all of this work was going on, Charles was getting more deeply involved with Mary Morris. He was still disappointed that he had been unable to convince Mary to introduce him to her father. Then, one evening whilst in Tony's café with Mary, her father walked in. He was not surprised that the normal chatter in the café stopped markedly on his arrival. Then he sat down at their table, and opened up the conversation by saying, "All right Charlie, what have you to say for yourself?"

Charles took a deep breath and then said, "I am twenty years old. I live in Myrdle Street with my mother, I am a heavy goods driver, and work for Mr Jones in Cannon Street Road. I was at school with Mary, and I think I would like to marry her when I have settled into my work, and have the money." Quite a testimony!

It was now Mr Morris's turn to take a deep breath, and think. Then he said, "I like you son I know all about your family, and I know Dan Jones. He thinks the world of you. The trouble is that I am just a bit worried about your friendship with Jim Baker and his mates. Tell me about him. I know he is up to no good!"

Charles had been waiting for this one. "Well," he said, "Jim and I were at school together with Mary. I met him again after we left school, and we used to chat here in this café. That is all I know. He is just a friend."

"OK," said Mr Morris, "but before I answer your big question about Mary, just remember, I will be watching you. I have no objection to you taking Mary out, but please be careful, behave yourself, and do not get involved in whatever your friend Jim Baker is up to."

Charles thanked him for the warning, then continued by assuring Mr Morris that he had no intention of getting involved in whatever it was that Jim was up to. Furthermore, he only met or saw Jim Baker when he visited Tony's café, and his only reason for going there these days was to meet Mary. This seemed to satisfy Mr Morris, but at the same time Charles was aware of the fact that he could not be seen in Jim's company again at any other location, including the slaughter.

Elsewhere, whilst that last conversation was going on, Peter decided that nothing would be lost if he and Jim kept observation in Jamaica Road, for a week from 8am to noon. He also said that if the right vehicle should turn up, he wanted to check over the cab ignition wiring so that he would know how long it would take to hot wire it. On the Tuesday, the second day of the watch a large Ford, covered vehicle arrived in Jamaica Road, bearing the name of a famous biscuit company on its side. The driver got out, and walked about 50 yards to some offices and went inside. Peter walked to the lorry and managed to get the driver's door open. He then climbed in and shut the door behind him.

After about five minutes, he returned to Jim and the van. As far as Peter was concerned, the lorry presented no difficulty. He could hot wire it in a few minutes, but they would need Bert Hinchcliffe to drive it. Furthermore, Bert would have to be there when it was decided to take it. This was clearly the delivery that had been suggested in the information they had received.

It was 20 minutes before the driver returned to the vehicle. He was seen to leave the offices he had entered earlier, and now had in his hands a large buff envelope, which undoubtedly contained the documentation he had been there for. It was then decided that they would follow the lorry for a while to see which direction he took from Jamaica Road.

The driver had started the engine of his vehicle almost as soon as he had returned to his cab. He drove through Southwark to Kennington, turning right to get to Vauxhall, then over Vauxhall Bridge, where he turned left along the embankment towards Fulham. Clearly he was going westward, and it was decided that enough had been seen.

The next stop was Warrington Road. Bert was at his stall, and Peter went over to him to tell him of the latest ideas. Bert was pleased, and said that he could give it two days the following week, and it was agreed that he would meet Jim and Peter at the yard in Back Church Lane at 7.30am the following Monday.

Bert arrived at 7.30am on the Monday, as agreed, and they all got into the van and drove over Tower Bridge to Jamaica Road. They gave it until midday, but there was no sign of a vehicle that could have been the one that they were interested in. They returned to the yard, and bid Bert goodbye until the following morning.

Bert arrived once again sharp the next day. The trio got into the van, and drove to Tooley Street, where they parked up as before. At a quarter to nine the same lorry as had been seen the previous week arrived, it parked in the same place, and the driver got out as before, locked his cab and made his way to the office. Peter turned to Bert, and said, "Five minutes, give me five minutes, and then come over to the driver's side, and take the lorry to New Cross. We will get there first, and open up the slaughter for you."

Exactly five minutes later, Bert walked to the drivers side of the vehicle, let Peter out, started up the engine, and drove off. Peter walked back to the van and got in beside Jim, who drove off to Arlington Road. Ted Best had just arrived at his yard, as Peter entered, he then opened up the gateway or entrance to their Arch. Peter then walked back to the junction of Arlington Road, and Beckton Street, and waited.

He did not have to wait long before he saw Bert Hinchcliffe arrive with the lorry. He turned into the yard, and Peter locked the gates behind him. The next job was to empty the lorry. The Arch was clean and filling it presented no difficulty. In fact, it was just 11 o'clock when all of the cases of biscuits had been taken off and stacked up in the arch.

Turning to Bert, Peter said, "Your job is next on the list Bert. Get rid of that lorry. Somewhere up near Sur-

rey Docks should be all right. Then my friend, there is
the subject of the biscuits. I would think that will present
no problem to you with your knowledge of the market-
place. We will follow you, until you have dumped the
lorry, then we will take you back to your home ground."

Bert got back into the lorry, and drove out of the yard
Then, turning into Arlington Road, he made his way due
North, to Rotherhithe New Road. He parked the vehicle
in Plough Way. Removed Peters wiring, got out of the
cab, and walked over to the van which was now parked
opposite him. They then took Bert back to Warrington
Road, after agreeing to meet Bert at his stall at about
midday the following Monday. Bert had been in an ex-
ceedingly happy mood on this last journey. He felt that
the biscuits would go so fast, that he would need Jim,
Peter and their van for the following two days, to clear
the slaughter. Peter could not believe this, but at Bert's
insistence, they agreed to meet at New Cross the next
day.

At the meeting the following day, Bert had already
done his work, and done it well. Six van loads of biscuits had been spoken for, and the only person a little
worried was still Peter. He just could not believe that six
different people could keep their mouths shut about such
a windfall of stolen property. Bert, however, insisted
that these were people he had done business with over
the years, and they had never let him down to date.

Jim was not in the slightest bit worried. Bert had
proved himself with the last tinned meat job deliveries,
so Jim was quite prepared to go along with him on whatever he said, and assist with the deliveries. Bert was delighted to hear this, and slapping Jim on the back said,
"Right, come on then, let's get to the slaughter and start
moving the stuff."

John Swain

At Beckton Street, Peter got out and unlocked the gates. They then drove inside, and loaded up the van with cartons of biscuits. When the van was full, Jim said, "Right then, that's enough. Now where to Bert?"

"Raymouth Road," replied Bert.

They were met in Raymouth Road, by a friend of Bert Hinchcliffe who had a small car. "Follow me!" he shouted, and they drove behind him to a railway arch close by. Jim backed the van into the arch, and it was unloaded in a very few minutes. The man then handed Bert a large envelope and said, "That was what we agreed, Bert. Many thanks." Bert got back into the van and they returned to the arch in New Cross.

Peter was waiting for them by the gate, he opened it, they drove inside, and loaded up the van once more. Before they left, Peter handed Ted Best the envelope he had been given by Bert and said, "We will work this out while they" - indicating Bert and Jim in the van - "are away."

"Drummond Road, by Southwark Park," said Bert. They were on their way once again.

In Drummond Road, was another man in a car who, on seeing them arrive, got out of his vehicle, and walking over to the driver's side of the van said to Jim, "It's only round the corner from here, follow me." Jim did as he was asked, and sure enough it was only in a little side street, but there was a small lock-up garage there, a bit small for what was needed. The man got out and opened up the garage doors. For once Jim was a little disturbed at the openness of this drop. With small terraced houses so close by, surely someone could well see what was going on, and might well telephone the Police. He could not get the cartons off quick enough.

As it was, the delivery went off without incident, and when Bert got back into the van, Jim could not resist the desire to give vent to his thoughts. Bert, however, would have none of it. He had done business with these people over the years, and was quite happy in the thought that they, the people in the close vicinity, would never grass on him or any of his friends.

The return journey was uneventful, and on arrival in Beckton Street, Peter opened up the yard once again. Once inside, Bert went to Ted Best's arch, and tossed another large envelope over for him to look after. Peter and Jim then commenced loading up the van once again. When it was full, Bert called over to Jim, "Let's get rid of this one quick." As they approached Arlington Road, Bert said "Southwark Street, this time over near London Bridge. In Southwark Street, Bert told Jim to stop. He got out of the van and went over to a public house in one of the side streets. He returned after a couple of very long minutes. Jim was sweating profusely.

Bert beckoned Jim to drive the van and stop by the side of the public house. As he stopped, the door was opened from the inside, and a man came out and assisted Bert to get the cartons out of the van. They then piled them up inside the passage of the private entrance of the public house. Jim was still in something of a cold sweat. He felt that he was walking on very thin ice. With all of the traffic in Southwark Street, only round the corner, and the odd vehicle passing by as the unloading was going on. He could not believe that someone would not cause the Police to arrive on the scene in double quick time. It seemed quite unnatural to him.

Jim had no desire to show himself as being scared, but in the circumstances, he felt quite justified in expressing his anxiety and feelings. Bert accepted his words in the sense that they were given, but went on to explain his actions more fully. He only dealt with people he had known for many years, he reassured Jim, people he went to school with and families he knew intimately.

There was still a few cases of biscuits left in the arch, and Peter, turning to Bert said, "I think we should to clear this arch out."

Jim reluctantly agreed saying, "I think we have been sailing a bit close to the wind lately, and should give it a rest for a while, but that's up to you."

Bert chipped in with, "We will clear out the arch, there is not much there, but I can drop the lot off in no time at all. Why don't you come along as well Jim?" Jim agreed, for in truth, he had little choice.

After emptying the contents of the arch into the van, Jim got into the driver's seat, and said, "Where to Bert?"

"Along the Old Kent Road, to Dunton Street, and right at the lights there," replied Bert.

As they approached Dunton Roads, he slowed down and turned right. "Rolls Road," said Bert, "second on the right along here."

As he set his indicator to turn right, a man jumped out from the pavement, and shouted to Bert as he jumped on to the running board of the van. "For Christ sake don't go down there! The heavy mob are all over Foxy's yard and will stop anything moving that they fancy."

Jim was truly shaken whilst Bert seemed as cool and calm as the proverbial cucumber. His friend 'Jacko' was busy enquiring what he might have on board. "Biscuits," said Bert.

"Right," said Jacko, "I know a publican just off Grange Road who will have them if its not too many, and what I see seems only a small load for you."

As directed, they stopped outside the George public house and Jacko got out and entered. After a few minutes the nearby cellar flap opened, and Bert opened up the back of the van and passed the cases of biscuits to Jacko, who promptly handed them down to someone below. Jacko then waved his hand to them, and called out, "See you later Bert, be lucky!"

Jim drove the van back to Beckton Street. He was having some difficulty controlling himself. He had never been quite so shaken up before. "Who the devil was that Jacko, Bert?" he asked.

"Oh, just a good friend," replied Bert. "Here's the money for those biscuits, and I have given Jacko his whack. He certainly earned it. The last people we want to get involved with is the heavy mob."

At Beckton Street, Peter was standing by and opened up the gates. They dove the van back into the yard, and parked it inside the arch, then closed it down. Jim and Bert, together with Peter, then went into Ted Best's arch, and sat down for a discussion on what had taken place. It was agreed all round that Jim and Bert had been very lucky. It was also agreed that Bert had excellent contacts who could warn him of the probable danger of stopping outside the Rolls Road yard. Yes, Foxy would have his delivery when it all settled down, and a suitable place had been found, but it was up to Bert to sort the matter out as he alone knew the man who had prevented what could have been a disaster.

The greatest worry that Peter had was whether Bert had dropped any of the tinned meat in the Rolls Road yard before, and whether whoever had 'shopped' his friend's neighbour had seen him make a delivery there.

Bert, however, was happy that his friend known in the area as 'Foxy Jones' did not have a delivery of tinned meat. Furthermore, he had not been in his yard for some months.

Bert was quite adamant, however, that he would not go near either to 'Foxy' or his friends yard for a long while, his reasoning being that if the heavy mob - Flying Squad - had had success at his neighbour's yard, and they liked the look of the area, they would in all probability keep at least a casual observation on the vicinity for some while. Furthermore, their casual observations were anything but casual!

In a final effort to put the others at ease, Bert hastened to assure them that he would be speaking to a reliable contact that evening. He was quite satisfied in his own mind that the contact would come up with a safe alternative slaughter for the remaining load, with payment on delivery. Furthermore, Fred Jones had not earned his nickname 'Foxy' for nothing

The shock of the near miss with the Rolls Road load seemed to register more strongly with Jim and Peter than with Bert, who accepted the situation in a quite nonchalant manner. His whole attitude was: It's Them and Us. 'Us' were in it to make money, and to make money, we had to steal, and then sell to people who did not have the bottle to steal themselves. That was the first weak link in our line of communication. 'Them' were the Police, who were in business to catch 'Us', the thieves, and also the recipients of stolen property. The Police were fortunately at a disadvantage, because they did not have those proverbial crystal balls to gaze into. To learn who was stealing or receiving the vast quantities of regularly stolen property, they had to rely on information from paid informants, careless talk, or lengthy observations.

They obtained their information mostly by either paying people who had fallen on hard times, or listening to stories relayed to them by criminals who want revenge on their associates. This applied particularly when the said criminals have entered into an agreement to do an unlawful act, and have not received what they consider just payment for carrying out that act.

Bert continued by mentioning that there were also times when the Police hear that such and such a type of stolen property is being sold in a particular area. In those cases, they generally set up observations in the area, and usually end up arresting someone for stealing or receiving property belonging to someone else. Both Jim and Peter listened intently to Bert's dissertation on the activities of the Police. He seemed to have a lot of the answers, and certainly had many useful contacts.

Then Peter turned to Bert and said, "If what you say is true, we are wasting our time, and sooner or later we will get ourselves arrested."

Bert nodded sagely at Peter's little outburst. He was clearly worried himself about the near miss situation that had occurred. He then said to Peter, "You decided to take up a life of crime. You must therefore be aware of the risks. There is no such thing as the perfect crime, irrespective of what newspapers and books may tell you. As a criminal, you are just a gambler, some you win, and although I don't like saying it, some you lose. We are already lucky, because if that friend of mine had not stopped us as we were turning into Rolls Road, we might all have been nicked."

The meeting broke up with a general agreement between all present that they must be more careful in the future. Bert insisted that he would arrange for the next load of biscuits, or whatever, to be taken to whoever Foxy nominated, and would call at the yard in Back Church Lane the following morning with the news.

On the return journey by public transport, Peter expressed his dislike of travelling by bus. Bert laughed and said that he would be getting off in the Old Kent Road, shortly, but would be up at their yard in the morning. Bert arrived in Back Church Lane, at 11 o'clock the following morning, and was full of the joys of spring. He had an address in Catford, way off their normal patch, where he would be able to leave the remaining biscuits. Jim and Peter then got into his van, and he drove them over to New Cross.

Once in Beckton Street, Peter went into the yard. Ted Best was in his arch working away on the engine of a vehicle. Peter told him that the last load would be taken out. He then signalled to Bert to leave his van in the yard, and opened up the third arch for Jim to get the last load out.

Outside the yard, Bert got into the passenger seat, and said to Jim, "Brownhill Road, Catford, do you know it?" Jim nodded, and dove off.

Once in Brownhill Road, Bert directed Jim to turn into one of the side roads. There he told Jim to stop outside a public house. Bert went inside but returned a few minutes later to stamp on the cellar flap near where the van had stopped. The cellar flap was then opened from the inside, and Bert went to the back of the van and took out cartons of biscuits which he pushed down the loading ramp inside the opening. When the van was empty, Bert went inside the public house. He returned a few minutes later, and patting his jacket, said, "All paid on" as he got back into he van.

The Van Draggers

CHAPTER 6
BIG BUSINESS IN RADIOS

They returned to Beckton Street, where they all gathered round for the big payout. It had worked out as a 'monkey' apiece, as they had previously estimated. Not a bad job despite the little scare! After a handshake all round, the group broke up, leaving Ted Best to his car repairs, and the peaceful surroundings of a yard that now had nothing to hide.

Jim was still worried about Peter's little outburst the previous day. He attempted to induce him to express this feelings, now that he had a pocket full of money. As far a he could get, however, was to learn that Peter was quite happy with the way things had worked out, but insisted that every care must be taken in the future because that Rolls Road stop was a very near miss, never to be repeated.

The logic expressed by Bert and Peter could not be ignored. The trio had been very fortunate so far, and as far as Jim was concerned, he was going to be very careful in the future. He had never really got over the shock of the fellow who had jumped out in front of the van as they were turning to drive into Rolls Road, just a few yards from disaster.

Once back in the yard, Peter said to Jim, "I think I will find a nice little Ford for Ted Best to play with. We can't earn big money from cars that way, but it will keep the landlord happy, and it will keep Ted occupied. At least we do have a great slaughter Jim, and I think we will need it soon. I still have a few interesting irons in the fire."

To Jim, this statement confirmed that Peter was not thinking of breaking up the partnership, and even if he was only thinking of the odd Ford motor car for Ted to get rid of, it meant that they were still in business. They finally agreed to meet again in two days' time. Peter felt sure that he would have 'something' lined up by then, and would probably want Jim to take him for a ride in the van.

Friday came and Peter still had no new job lined up, but he fancied a curry. He called in at the yard as arranged, and he and Jim went off to Hell's Kitchen. Simon was delighted to see them again, and told them that Fred Stone should be in any minute.

Halfway through the curry, Fred arrived. His first words were, "Good to see you two, but I don't suppose you would be interested in radios, Peter?" What a question!

"Right now, Fred, we would be interested in anything," replied Peter.

"Great," said Fred. "This is going to cost you a tun at least, just for the story."

Fred collected his curry from Simon, and sat down with Jim and Peter. He then began to recount his regular meetings with one of his friends, a lorry driver who just loved curry. This driver apparently worked for an electronic company in Colchester. Every week he had to take a lorry to Newhaven. He would board the ship with his vehicle, then drive to somewhere in France, returning the following day to Newhaven. Then it was home to Colchester the same day as he landed.

This character, according to Fred, just loved Simon's

80

Curry. His passage was booked from Newhaven to Dieppe for every Thursday. He would arrive in Limehouse just before noon, park his lorry close to Fred's yard, then look in on him, and they would come round to Simon's and have a curry. They were always there for about an hour, after which the lorry driver drove off, not to be seen until the following week.

His load usually consisted of transistor radios, mostly from the Far East, and some articles manufactured by the company in Colchester. "We are interested," said Peter, "but if you could delay him for another hour at least, we will double the tun."

This presented no difficulty to Fred Stone. He was very much aware that the driver, on finding his vehicle missing, would immediately come into his yard, and ask if anything had been seen or heard. Fred would then take the driver for a drive round the district to see if it had been dumped locally, before taking him into Limehouse Police Station to report the matter.

By now the meals had been finished. They each shook hands, and Peter assured Fred Stone that everything would be arranged and taken care of. He also assured him that he would be well looked after in due course.

As they drove away from Limehouse, both Jim and Peter were delighted with the day's work. How often in life do such opportunities arise when nothing is planned further than a meal or drink in pleasant surroundings?

The first call was to New Cross. Ted Best was working away on one his favourite Ford motor cars. Peter told him that they were expecting some good news in about a week, and that they intended cleaning up the arch. In truth, there was nothing much they could do. They did check over the hinges that took the strain of the two

John Swain

large doors, and swept up the interior. After about five minutes, however, they closed up the arch once again, bid Ted a cheery goodbye, and left.

They got back into the van, and drove down Arlington Road. As they moved off, Peter said, "Stop at the off licence by the pub, Jim, and I will go in and get a bottle of Scotch. Then we will go down to Kent, and talk with our farmer friend."

With the bottle of whisky safely in the van, they continued on their way to Kent. As they stopped by the barn, the farmer appeared out of the blue. He had not been seen as they drove in, but he just suddenly appeared beside them.

"Good to see you," said Peter. "We were just passing through, and thought we would bring in this bottle to crack with you. We feel a little thirsty ourselves, and you supplied the drink last time."

The farmer was obviously very pleased to see the boys, and invited them into his farmhouse once again, and a good time was had by all. This farmer could certainly drink, perhaps it was all the heavy work he did, or perhaps he was a regular drinker, which neither Jim or Peter were. The fact of the matter was that the bottle was very soon empty and deposited in a bin at the fireside.

During the course of the conversation whilst the Scotch was being disposed of, mention had been made that a delivery was expected, but they could not give an exact date of it. The farmer was pleased to hear this. He did not want to know the date of the delivery, but repeated what he had said on the previous visit.

"The barn is yours, just drive in when you are ready, and cover up whatever it is. That canvas cover is still there." This was a most satisfactory arrangement, and after finishing off what was left of their drink, the two lads drove out of the farm.

Once on the main road, Peter asked Jim where he was going next. There could not be much doubt about that. Jim let out a quiet chuckle, and said, "Warrington Road. We have some business to discuss with Bert Hinchcliffe, don't you think?"

Peter thumped Jim on the back, and said, "Right on, mate!"

At Warrington road, Bert was just about to pack up his stall. He was pleased to see the lads and when they asked him to keep the following Thursday free, he agreed to be at the Back Church Lane yard at 7am that day. He fully understood what he would probably have to do, and mentioned that he would first of all check over his route from Rotherhithe Tunnel to the farm in Kent. Peter told him not to worry too much because he had not been to the Kent slaughter. All he would have to do on the day was to follow the van that he knew so well, which would contain Jim and Peter.

Once back in the yard, it was agreed that the following week would be a quiet one, and nothing was arranged until the meeting on Thursday morning. Peter was happy that he could hot wire whatever vehicle arrived that day, and they would have probably two hours before the balloon went up.

Bert Hinchcliffe arrived at the yard with his usual promptness at a quarter to seven on the Thursday morning. Peter arrived a few minutes later, carrying a small folding chair. He expressed his dislike of travelling with three people in the front of a van. He thought it was an activity that could attract Police attention, and should not be continued.

Peter was of course right, particularly on a day when of necessity three people might well have to remain in the stationary van for a number of hours. This pleased Peter, and confirmed Bert's wise move of bringing his folding seat with him. He could thus sit out of sight in the back of the van.

Fred Stone's yard was in the road that was almost at the rear of Simon's restaurant, and parking the van within sight of the yard was not difficult. The only trouble being that Jim was obliged to pull up on to the pavement in order to allow traffic to pass by.

True to form, a large Ford Box van arrived at a quarter past twelve, and parked on the pavement outside Fred's yard. The driver got out, locked the door, and kicked the corrugated iron fence of Fred's yard. He called out something, then walked round the corner and into West India Dock Road. Fred Stone was then seen to leave his yard, and follow on behind the driver who was now out of sight.

Peter got out of the van and, turning to Bert said, Give me five minutes!" and walked to the still warm Box van. He opened the door immediately, and got in. After about five minutes, Bert got out of the van, went to the Ford and entered the cab. Peter then got out as the vehicle engine started up. Jim started up, and followed on. In Commercial Road East, he was obliged to passed the Ford, and entered Rotherhithe Tunnel with that vehicle immediately behind him. Once out of the tunnel, the two vehicles then made a steady journey together with the van now leading the way, through the roads of Bermondsey, Catford, and Bromley, then on into the Kent countryside.

Bert stuck with the little van like glue, and was only a

few feet away from it as they turned into the farm roadway. As they stopped by the barn, Peter got out, and opened up the barn. He then directed Bert to drive right inside. This done, they all started to unload the contents of the Box van. It was quite a tidy haul, with everything contained in secure wooden boxes, and in the cab of the Box van a large envelope was found which set out everything that was in those boxes.

When the Box van was empty, Peter turned to Bert, and said, "You know your next job, Bert. Jim will follow you and pick you up when you have dumped the truck. Just keep going down the Hastings road here until you find somewhere you fancy. Then remove the wiring, as usual, and get into the van with Jim and come back here."

After about 20 miles Bert pulled into a large lay-by with no vehicles parked in it. From the oil traces on the ground, however, it was obviously a well used parking place. He climbed out of the cab and walked over to Jim. They both then returned to the farm. Peter opened up some of the wooden cases. Most of them contained small transistor radios, while some were full of spare parts, either for repair work, or perhaps for building your own radio, if you are a radio ham. Bert was very interested in the radios. "A bit specialised," he said, but there were one or two people he knew who might well be interested in them.

He would have to have a look round some of his contacts and see what sort of response he got. As to the boxes of spare parts, these were useless to them, and would have to be dumped somewhere. While the talk was going on, the farmer arrived in the barn. He heard mention that some of the spare parts would have to be dumped, and said that he thought he could assist. He was in the process of filling in an old sewage pit, and the parts not the boxes could be thrown in there. They would sink below the surface, and never be found. He always had a bonfire going for rubbish, so the boxes could go on there as soon as you like.

The farmer then took Peter out of the barn to show him the sewage pit that he was talking about. It was about 300 yards away, and as they got nearer, its presence became quite obvious. What a stink!

Returning to the barn, the farmer produced some plastic sacks and said, "Put the stuff you don't want in these, and throw the sacks in with the stuff, that way they will sink faster. Don't worry, the contents will never be seen again!"

The trio then opened up all of the cases. Only three had spare parts that had to be dumped, the remaining boxes all contained radios. These they put to one side, and covered them over with the canvas sheeting. They then loaded the spare parts into four sacks, carried them to the sewage pit, and threw them in. Despite the smell, they stood by and watched the sacks slowly sink below the surface and out of sight.

The next job was to break up the three wooden cases, and take the wood over to the bonfire that was still smouldering. After making sure that any markings had been properly obscured they put the documents and the envelope on the smouldering ashes. These soon lit up, and the wood and the documents became history as they went up in smoke.

After thanking the farmer, they all shook hands with him and made their way back to London. Bert drove his van out of the yard, and waved a cheery farewell as he left, promising to have some news for them in a day or so.

Two days later, Jim and Peter called over to see Bert at his stall. He had two orders for 50 radios at £5 each, so he would like them as soon as possible. It was agreed that they would be delivered to him before he closed later in the afternoon. They shook hands on the deal and drove off to Kent.

All was quiet at the farm, and they drove the van into the barn. There seemed to have been 250 radios in each case. They took out the required number, placing 50 in each of the five plastic sacks that they had retained in the barn after disposing of the spare parts on their last visit. These they placed in their van. Before leaving, Peter broke up the empty case, and took it over to the bonfire site. It was smouldering away as usual, and he threw pieces of wood into the apparently hottest part, and watched. Satisfied that it would soon be burnt beyond recognition, he turned back towards the barn. There was no sign of the farmer, so he decided to leave.

According to his reckoning, there were seven wooden cases left in the barn. Each case would probably contain 150 radios. They were therefore leaving behind something in the order of 1000-plus radios. Quite a haul! They must now be disposed of, and soon.

They drove back to Warrington Road, where Bert was busy on his stall. They said that they would like to see him at New Cross, and left. They told Ted Best that they were in business once again, and opened up their arch. They then placed the five sacks in the arch on a table that Peter had set up for the purpose when he built the gates for the archway.

It was an hour before Bert Hinchcliffe arrived. He drove into the yard, and two of the sacks were placed in his van. "Come and see me tomorrow morning," he said. "I may be able to tell you where to take some more. I think these will go like hot cakes."

When Bert had left, Peter was in a somewhat pensive mood. Jim tried to break the ice by asking what he had on his mind. Peter indicated that he was worried about the amount of stuff that was static down at the farm., and would be there for some while. He felt that a call over to Shepherds Bush would do no harm. They could at least take a sample over with them and see what Wally Fish had to say.

The following morning, as requested, Jim and Peter drove over to Warrington Road. Bert had no new information for them. Those who had taken the first two consignments wanted to see how they went, and this was also the general feeling amongst those who dealt in this type of commodity. Bert promised to keep in touch and to tell them as soon as any more were required. He did, however, hand over £500 as payment for the first 100 radios. From Walworth, Jim drove over to Shepherds Bush. Wally Fish was not hard to find, and he welcomed them with open arms. "What have you got for me now?" he asked.

Peter showed him the sample that he had brought from the farm. "We have about 500 of these, Wally. How much?" said Peter.

Wally examined it and said, "That's not fair to either of us. You tell me how much you want for each one, and we will see if we can do business."

"We want five pounds apiece," said Peter, "paid on delivery, and we do not haggle."

Wally Fish did not seem pleased, but he was a dealer, and was bound to try to cut them down. "I would not want to pay more than three and a half," said Wally.

"OK," said Peter, "perhaps some other time. We're off . Where shall we drop you?"

"Take me to the Green," said Wally.

Just short of Shepherds Bush Green, Wally asked Jim to stop the van and pull into the kerb. Here he further examined the radio, and finally said to Peter, "I will take 100 to see how they go, and here's a monkey, but I will pay on delivery."

It was agreed that they would meet Wally at the same place on the coming Saturday afternoon at about three o'clock. With that Wally got out of the van and left them.

The rest of the week was very quiet. Bert Hinchcliffe had not come back with further orders, so on the Saturday morning, Jim and Peter went to New Cross and loaded up the van with two plastic bags of radios, 50 in each. They then drove over to Shepherds Bush and met Wally as arranged. At his request, they followed him to a yard just off the Uxbridge Road. Wally opened the yard gates, and Jim drove the van inside. Here they received the promised £500 in cash from Wally Fish. They then shook hands and left. Before departing, however, they informed him that there were more if required. This obviously pleased Wally, but he only indicated that when the time was right, he would be on to them. He ended up by suggesting that perhaps they would care to call on him in two weeks' time to see how things were going.

Returning to the yard in Back Church Lane, Jim parked the van and walked round to Tony's café. Tony was delighted to see him, and said that things had been very quiet since they had stopped coming regularly.

Tony was in a very talkative mood and went on to tell Jim that his friend Charlie Burton came in about once a week with Mary Morris, and that on one occasion, her father had turned up, which gave the girl quite a fright. He was also convinced that they were going to become engaged very soon. Apparently Mary's father, Detective Sergeant Jim Morris had been was very much against this to start with, but he felt that Jim Morris had made his enquiries about Charlie, and now seemed happy with the pair of them. Charlie was still doing his heavy lorry driving, was well appreciated by his boss, and seemed very happy with things in general.

On the following Wednesday morning, Jim and Peter met up at the yard, and decided to pay a visit to Bert Hinchcliffe at his stall in Warrington Road. On their way Peter mentioned that there were some very interesting 'goings on' in the City of London that should be looked at. When a large van of interesting gear had broken down, the driver had left the vehicle to get help and on his return, found that it had been virtually emptied. Jim just laughed and said, "What do you expect?"

Peter insisted on going on with his story, mentioning that these characters first meet up with their own van, four-handed, then tour the busy City of London roads looking for an interesting heavy van that is loaded and stationary in a traffic jam. They then move their vehicle to a position behind that van as the traffic moves on. Then when it stops at the next block. One of the van draggers gets out and places a heavy inverted spike under one of the rear wheels of the target van. The inevitable happens as that van moves off, there is a puncture. The van driver stops to see what has happened, and one of the friendly van draggers takes the driver away to summon assistance whilst the remaining characters engage in either helping themselves to the contents of the van or

The Van Draggers

directing the traffic around the obstruction.

"What do you think of that?" said the bold Peter. "Sounds like something we could use."

"Not so bloody likely," replied Jim. "I bet they were all nicked."

"As a matter of fact they were," replied Peter, "but you must admit, it was a wonderful idea which we could improve on."

Nothing further was said on that matter, so they made their way to Warrington Road, where Bert was in his element, selling his wares to housewives. When the queue died down, they went over to him. "I've hit the button here," he said. "I think I've found something that all the women in the neighbourhood are looking for."

There was no visual indication as to what this wonder object was that all and sundry were anxious to purchase. Furthermore, neither Jim nor Peter wanted to be nosy and ask. If it was anything in their line of country, they knew Bert would tell them in his own time. As it was, Bert had no new enquiries or orders for more radios, so it seemed as if they would have to take it easy until the next order came in.

Peter decided to return to his love of buying and selling second hand motor cars. His Warren Street contacts were helpful on this count, and he was even able to get Jim to give him a hand delivering the odd vehicle.

Everything seemed so very quiet, but both of the lads had got used to the occasional limbo period. Fortunately, neither of them were heavy or habitual drinkers and spenders. They had enough money to live on without any worries at all, thanks to the fact that they always put cash from their work to one side for such times.

The time soon came round, however, when they were

due to call on Wally Fish again, so they made their way over to the Shepherds Bush area. Wally was, as usual, delighted to see them, which was always a good sign.. He wanted another hundred radios, and the sooner the better. They promised to fulfil this order probably the following day, and after shaking hands they left. On their way back to the yard in Back Church Lane, they decided that they would not go to the farm the following day, which would be Sunday, but would leave it until the day after, Monday. At the yard they agreed to meet there on Monday morning at ten.

They met as arranged and, after putting five plastic sacks in the van, they drove off to Kent. At the farm, all was quiet. They went into the barn, broke open a further case of radios and bagged them up 50 to a sack, then loaded the sacks again into the van, and were ready to go. Peter, however, had other things on his mind. "Wait a minute," he said. "I am going over to give the farmer some money. We can't keep him waiting for ever." Luckily, the farmer was at home, and was pleased to see Peter, even more so when Peter gave him £100 in cash.

Jim and Peter then made their way to New Cross. Ted Best was there working away on a small van. They waved to him as they drove in and went to their arch. There they took out three of the sacks, and placed them inside the arch. They then closed it up again, and prepared to leave. Jim then went over to Ted and gave him £100, saying, "That's part payment, Ted. There's more to come in due course." They then shook hands, and Jim went back to the van and drove off.

The next stop was Wally Fish's yard off the Uxbridge Road. He likewise was pleased to see them, but complained because they had not turned up the previous day, as they had indicated on the Saturday visit. Peter, however, muttered something about it being wrong to call over with goods on a Sunday. This caused Wally to roar with laughter, and the pressure was off them. He then dipped into his very deep pockets, and produced £500 in a roll, secured with the time honoured elastic bands, and handed it over to Peter.

On their way back to the East End of London, Jim suggested that they should go over to Limehouse for a curry. "Not a bad idea," said Peter. "Let's see if Simon has emptied his curry cauldron yet. If not, we'll empty it for him - I'm bloody hungry!"

At Hell's Kitchen, Simon was delighted to see them, and passed over a healthy portion of curry for each of them. Then to their surprise, he came over and sat with them. Simon expressed his concern about Fred Stone. He indicated that the police had been very interested in him since that lorryload of radios had been nicked in Limehouse. They had been worth a hell of a lot of money, and Fred had been questioned by the Police for some time about their disappearance.

At that moment, there was a call from above. "Are you there, Simon?"

"Down here," replied Simon. "I've got some friends of yours here."

Fred then came trotting down the stairs. On seeing Jim and Peter, he said, "Oh Jeez, you two! You should keep away from here, and keep to your own patch." He then sat with them, and a plate of curry was put in front of him.

CHAPTER 7
THE END OF AN ERA.

The Limehouse C.I.D., had taken Fred in for questioning after the Box van of radios had been stolen. They had kept him in the station until midnight. To use Fred's words: "It was quite a performance." But he knew nothing about the theft, in fact it was as the driver had explained, he was with Fred right from the time he had parked his van and entered Simon's for a curry. According to the C.I.D., Fred had to know something about the theft, but after keeping him for some time at the station, they finally gave up and let him go.

The van driver had not been back in the area since. No doubt he had found another route, or perhaps they found another driver for the job. Jim gave Fred £50, and thanked him for not mentioning anything that could involve them. Fred thanked him for the cash, but suggested it might be as well if they kept away from Limehouse for a while. With that, Jim and Peter shook hands with Fred and left.

They walked round the corner from Simon's restaurant to Grenade Street, where Jim had parked his van, and drove off. Peter was surprised to find that they were driving through Rotherhithe Tunnel, instead of keeping on the north side of the river and driving through Shadwell. When he mentioned this, Jim reminded him that as they had just left Simon's restaurant, which was right opposite Limehouse Police Station, they might be connected with Fred and the van theft, and followed. For that reason, he had decided to take the indirect route home. Once in their yard at Back Church Lane, they relaxed a little, but decided to take things a little easy in future.

Meanwhile, in deepest Kent, the farmer had received a visit from the Kent Police. They had never closed the case of the stolen lorryload of cigarettes, and were still making routine enquiries of people in the area. The farmer was most surprised when he found himself being questioned about a local incident that must have taken place two years ago.

He invited them to inspect anywhere on his farm, and offered every assistance he could think of, short of taking them over to the barn. The Police finally left, delighted to have had a small glass of Scotch with the farmer, and apologising most profusely for taking up his valuable time. They returned to their cars, but on their way back to the station, decided amongst themselves that the farmer was lying. He had been just too helpful.

At a conference in the Police Station that evening, the Detective Inspector who had originally dealt with the theft was pleased to hear how his men felt in relation to the farmer. His farm was quite near to the scene of that offence. Also, it was sufficiently secluded to support a useful observation plan. He also felt it would be a good idea if one of his men had a quiet unofficial look into some of his outbuildings that had not been examined.

The following morning, Detective Constable George Brown set out on his motor cycle to work out a plan of campaign. He did not know whether the farmer had dogs that roamed around at night, and did not want to bring the dogs down on himself while he was snooping around. The officer could see no evidence of dogs, and decided to return that night after dark, and see if he could find anything of interest.

It was just after one o'clock in the morning when he returned. The farmhouse was in darkness, and he decided to have a look at the first outbuilding, the barn on the road into the farm itself. He found the door secured by a bolt passed through a lock hasp. Lifting out the bolt, he was able to pull the door back sufficiently to enter. There was a plough in one corner, and something under a tarpaulin cover on one side. He lifted the cover, and found a wooden case with some numbers on it, and an address in France. He noted these particulars, closed back the cover and left, after placing the bolt back in its original position.

Later that morning, Detective Constable Brown typed out his report and handed it to his Detective Inspector, who, needless to say, was delighted. This was good news indeed. It seemed as if they had at least found 'something'. He therefore gave orders for his men to get a search warrant, and search the farm and all outbuildings that day.

Just before midday, a dozen Kent officers arrived at the farm and, accompanied by the farmer, carried out a full search. Their first stop was the barn. Under the canvas cover, they found the cases of radios. The farmer could think of no explanation why these should be there. He was arrested.

A Police Tender was sent for, and the cases and radios loaded on board. The Detective Inspector then got his men together to spread out the canvas cover. He let out a whoop of joy. It bore the name of he haulage company that had lost the cigarettes so long ago - a job that was nevertheless still fresh in his mind because of its serious nature. The canvas cover was also loaded on to the Police Tender, and the party left, having found nothing further. They also took the farmer, who was still professing his ignorance of the whole matter.

Once at the Police Station, the Detective Inspector got out his old papers on the cigarette theft. There he found the details of Peter Ginsberg, who had been brought in for questioning, but had to be released due to lack of concrete evidence against him. He let out a quiet chuckle, lifted up the telephone and called Detective Sergeant Jim Morris at Leman Street Police Station. Hadn't he said on the previous occasion that he knew Ginsberg? How very interesting!

Morris was delighted to hear from the Kent Police on the matter. He was well aware that he had no evidence against either Ginsberg or his mate Jim Baker. Nevertheless, he still felt in his bones that they were up to no good. Now he had good reason to do something about it. Morris knew that they had a yard at Back Church Lane, and had been inside it when there was nobody there. He had never found anything suspicious there, and had therefore left it alone. Now he was going to set up an observation on the yard, and see what they were up to in there.

The first two days were a waste of time. He had put two men on the railway line watching Back Church Lane. There had been no visitors to the yard used by the two suspects. He was not convinced, so he decided to keep the observation on until they were sighted, for he knew in his heart that they must come there. The van that they used was still in the yard, and had not been moved.

Jim Morris was no fool, but with the equipment he had available in those days, he had bitten off a little more than he could chew. He had a Hillman Minx motor car at the station, and kept that back for use in connection with the observation. He was aware that it was a known Police vehicle, but had radio contact with his men on the railway line. Thus when he received a call that the suspects had arrived at the yard, he got into his Hillman and drove to Back Church Lane.

He saw the van leave the yard, and kept it in sight until it had gone over Tower Bridge. He followed down Tower Bridge Road, to the Elephant and Castle, then along Walworth Road. The van suddenly stopped at Warrington Road, turned in and parked just round the corner.

Jim Morris parked up in the main road, and left the car. He crossed to the other side of the road, and looked up Warrington Road. He saw the suspects stop and talk to a stallholder, so decided to wait and see just how long they would be there.

It was some 20 minutes before the two suspects returned to their vehicle. They turned the van in the narrow road, and returned to the Walworth Road. They turned left, and then left again into Albany Road, right into Wells Way and left into Southampton Way. Ultimately they arrived at the Old Kent Road, where they turned into Arlington Road. There they took the first turning on the right, into Beckton Street. As Morris got parallel with this road, he saw the van parked outside a yard. He carried on for a few yards, got out and walked back. The two suspects were in the process of driving into a yard hidden by some fairly high corrugated iron fencing. Morris felt that it was time he turned for home.

He had been exceptionally lucky so far, but such luck could not remain with him all of the time.

Back at Leman Street Police Station, he telephoned the Flying Squad office, and asked for his friend, Detective Inspector Tommy Hutchins. Tom was out on patrol, and the operator said that he would call him up on the radio, and get him to ring Morris at Leman Street. Morris was frustrated about the delay, but there was nothing he could do but wait. With a cup of tea in front of him, he strummed his desk top with his fingers. Questions kept coming to his mind. Should he have steamed into the yard and attempted to keep the two men there? No, that would have been stupid. He did not know who else was in the yard and could have got himself beaten up and lost the suspects completely. That would have been a real disaster.

At that moment, the telephone rang. It was Tommy Hutchins. "What's all the hurry?" said Tommy.

"You'd better come over here as quick as you can. Our van draggers are at it again and I think I have a good job for you. It may even go out as far as Kent," said Morris.

"We are in Golders Green at the moment," said Hutchins, "and will be with you in a half hour, subject to traffic."

It was three quarters of an hour before Tom Hutchins arrived at Leman Street Police Station. He sat down with Jim Morris, and listened with great interest to his story. "You did the right thing leaving it alone," said Hutchins. "I think you would probably have fouled the job up if you had steamed in there. You were not to know how many there were in the yard, and you were alone. Full marks for using your loaf, and leaving when you did."

Jim Morris then went with the Flying Squad officers to Walworth. There he indicated the stallholder that the two suspects had spoken to. One of the officers present knew the man as Bert Hinchcliff who had a conviction for receiving stolen property a few years earlier. The next stop was Arlington Road, New Cross. They passed Beckton Street and stopped. One of the officers then got out and walked back. He turned into Beckton Street, and had a look through a joint in the corrugated iron fencing.

He returned to the car and said that he thought that there was nobody in the yard. Also, there was no sign of a van in the yard. "Don't worry," said Detective Inspector Hutchins. "I will set up an observation here, somewhere out of sight, and we will have these characters as soon as they show up. They should come along in the van that you mentioned, and we have the index number. Now, in the meantime, how about a trip down to Kent? I know the Detective Inspector who dealt with that big cigarette job down there a few years back."

"It was Detective Sergeant Walter Graham, who had young Ginsberg in on that matter," said Jim Morris.

"That's the man," said Hutchins. "He's the man we will have to speak to. He's a Detective Inspector now."

At Sevenoaks Police Station they soon located Graham. He was pleased to see them, and told them that he was just going to telephone Limehouse Police Station. He had just located some of the radios that had been stolen in Limehouse a few weeks ago.

"Don't bother to ring them yet," said Hutchins, "This is something that is best if I deal with them and you. The Limehouse Officers are tied to their division, whilst on the Flying Squad we have a roving commission. Detective Inspector Graham then outlined to those present just what had taken place at the farm, including the fact that they had seized over 100 transistor radios, and the tarpaulin cover from the stolen lorry. Finally, he told them that he now had the farmer in custody, and that he wanted to talk. He had so much to lose.

Jim Morris then mentioned his thoughts about Peter Ginsberg, who Kent Police had interviewed respecting the cigarette theft. He also mentioned Jim Baker, Ginsberg's close friend and associate, and that he felt they would both be arrested very shortly. The big thing was that they did not want to frighten them in any way. Certainly they did not want any publicity about the arrest of the farmer in the press, because that could spoil everything.

Graham agreed that he would do his best to prevent any press publicity, but pointed out that he would be obliged to charge the farmer with receiving the radios found in his barn, and the tarpaulin from the cigarette lorry. He mentioned that he felt sure that if they were able to arrest Ginsberg and his mate for a criminal offence, the farmer would probably be more helpful, as he was already teetering on the brink of being prepared to attend an identification parade.

Hutchins finally shook hands with Graham, and said that he would return to London and set up an observation in the hope of catching the two suspects red-handed in the near future. He also asked Graham to delay charging the farmer as long as was legally possible, in the interests of ultimate justice, because he felt sure he would be successful.

Observation was kept on the yard at the foot of Beckton Street from seven o'clock the following morning. An observation was also kept on the stallholder in Warrington Road. The old man Ted Best was seen to come to the yard in the morning, and return to his house in Arlington road at midday. He returned to the yard at two o'clock and did not leave until five, when he returned home. As for the stallholder, he arrived at his pitch at half past eight in the morning, and did not leave until five o'clock. Not a good result, but those engaged in keeping observation know full well that much of the time is waiting time, and there is so often nothing to show for the effort.

The following day, in addition to the watch in Warrington Road, and Beckton Street, they also watched the yard in Back Church Lane. At nine o'clock the following morning, Jim Baker arrived in the yard, started up the van, and waited. Ten minutes later, Peter Ginsberg arrived and got into the passenger seat. Jim drove off and was followed at a distance by one of the Flying Squad vehicles. They went straight to Warrington Road. Bert Hinchcliffe was not at his stall, so they waited in the van. Hinchcliffe arrived about a quarter of an hour later, and he also got into the van.

The van was then driven to Arlington Street, turned into Beckton Street, and parked. Peter Ginsberg got out and opened up the gates, Jim Baker drove into the yard, and Ginsberg closed the gates. The Flying Squad officers decided to wait.

They were only there for a few minutes when the yard gates opened once more, and Jim Baker drove the van into the street. Peter Ginsberg closed up the yard gates, and got into the van. In Arlington Road, about 200 yards from the yard, the Flying Squad vehicles stopped the van.

In the back sat Hinchcliffe, with two sacks of radios.

The Van Draggers

Neither wanted to say anything apart from demanding to be able to contact their solicitor. They were told that they would have to wait for that privilege. The prisoners were split up between three squad vehicles, and one of the officers drove the van. They all then made their way to Sevenoaks Police Station, where Detective Inspector Walter Graham was delighted to see them. He had been obliged to charge the farmer, and would be doing that later in the day. He decided first to interrogate the prisoners independently with one of the Flying Squad officers, Detective Inspector Hutchins, present.

The officers were hardly surprised when told that they were not going to say a word until their solicitor, Mr Lewis, arrived. They were permitted to telephone him, and prepared themselves to settle down and await his arrival. They were, however, cautioned, and certain questions were put to them, with their negative responses noted.

As far as the officers were concerned, it made little difference that the prisoners were not going to talk. They had been seen to go to the yard in Arlington Road, and were stopped as they left. What they did not know was that other Squad officers had entered the yard after they had been taken away, and searched the arch. They had taken possession of two further sacks of identical radios. Furthermore, Ted Best, the owner of the yard, was being brought to Sevenoaks by the officers.

There was no point at that stage in further questioning the prisoners from the van; they clearly thought it best to say nothing, and intended waiting for their solicitor. Ted Best, however, was questioned. He gave the firm impression of being unaware of whatever the three prisoners were up to. He had let the arch in his yard to Baker and Ginsberg to do repairs. He knew nothing about them, and did not want to know what they had in the arch which was secured by Ginsberg. A lengthy statement was taken from him, and he gave an undertaking to give evidence in accordance with his statement, if so required.

Detective Inspectors Graham and Hutchins then decided to have a chat with the farmer. He wanted to talk, and had not asked to see a solicitor. He was cautioned, and told that he need not say anything unless he wished to do so, and that whatever he did say would be taken down in writing, and might be given in evidence. He was quite happy, and told them of the meeting with Baker and Ginsberg, whom he knew only as Jim and Peter. They had called on him and asked if they could use his barn to store some of their goods. They had given him a total of £150 since they met, and he had not bothered to ask what they were storing in his barn, or for that matter to look at whatever was under the tarpaulin. They had paid in cash for the use of the barn, and he did not want to get involved in their business, whatever it was.

At a subsequent identification parade, the farmer, who was not charged, identified Hinchcliffe, Baker and Ginsberg. All were in due course dealt with in accordance with the law, and sentenced to long terms of imprisonment.

The most important criticism that came out from the subsequent trial was the fact that these men were able to get into the vehicles they stole with ease, and hot wire them without causing any alarm. Such criticisms that were obviously noted by high value haulage contractors, and vehicle manufacturers. The result was that such vehicles now have both cab alarms and vehicle immobilisers fitted to prevent the style of thefts that were so prevalent in the years just after the last war.

The Van Draggers

During the period between the first hearing in Kent at the Magistrates Court, and the subsequent trial at Crown Court, the Flying Squad had many successes, including the fact that some of the radios were appearing on stalls at Shepherds Bush Market. They arrested a number of recipients of stolen property, including Wally Fish at Shepherds Bush. In fact the final result in this case tended to prove that the long arm of the law usually manages to reach out to and arrest the van draggers on the other side of the fence.

CHAPTER 8
A NEW LIFE BEGINS

Business at Tony's café in Cable Street went on very much as before. There had been a period of uncertainty following the arrest of Jim Baker, probably because some of the customers had purchased 'cheap lines' from him and his friend Peter Ginsberg. Generally speaking, however, it was a case of business as usual for most of the regulars.

Charles did not change his mode of life in any way whatsoever. He was so grateful that he'd had the good sense in the past to disassociate himself from his erstwhile friends. He was also happy in the knowledge that he was enjoying his work as a respected and trusted heavy goods driver, and got on so well with his boss Dan Jones.

At home, in his days of relaxation, he would often sit and think back to the early days, to the almost Dickensian style of his introduction to crime by that modern day Fagin, Jim Baker, who had taken him out to show him how to steal from shop counters. He recalled his important driving lessons from Peter Ginsberg and the later experience that produced. This included how he had driven a stolen van believing in his heart, and as he was told at the time, that it belonged to Peter.

It was quite a catalogue of incidents that he had been innocently led into by his friend Jim Baker, now in prison along with Peter Ginsberg and others, for very serious crimes indeed. These contemplations did not cease. Charles thought so often of how near he had come to becoming a confirmed thief and van dragger like his one-time associates. If he had, he would probably now be a prisoner like his friends. These thoughts always ended up in the same manner, with him sitting back and looking up at the ceiling of the family flat in Myrdle Street, and thanking the Good Lord for his guidance in a time of dire need, which he had not appreciated at the time.

These periods of contemplation did not escape the notice of Mrs Burton. To her, it was something of a worry, because Charles had always been on the move in the past, and rarely sat silently in the flat just thinking. Clearly her son had something on his mind, and she had to find out what it was. She had asked him on a number of occasions, but never had been able to get a straight answer.

Then, to her complete surprise, he told her how, shortly after he had left school, he had been taken out by his friend Jim Baker and shown how to steal from shops. He also told her that, although he was grateful to Peter Ginsberg for teaching him how to drive, he knew that if he had continued his close association with those two, he would have ended up with them as just another van dragger in jail.

It was clear to Mrs Burton that undoubtedly Charles had been very much involved with his two friends, and her gratitude for his ending contact with them was clearly demonstrated by her tears of joy. She told him how glad she was that he was now following in his father's footsteps with a regular job at his dad's old firm. Then, after a long pause, she asked him if he had any further plan for the future.

He confirmed once again how satisfied he was with his life as a driver, and that he regarded it as a job for life. As to the future, he wanted to marry Mary Morris, who worked as a clerk in the bank up at the High Street. Mary was in agreement, but wanted to be sure first of all that her father, who was a Detective Sergeant at Leman Street Police Station, supported her intentions.

Mrs Burton supported Charles' decision, but thought that first of all he should bring Mary home for a quiet evening on Saturday. She added that she wanted to be sure Mary was the right sort of girl for him. This was agreed upon, and Charles decided there and then that he would attempt to set up such a visit as soon as possible.

Two days later, the couple met at Tony's café. Mary was delighted to hear of the invitation. She also mentioned then that she had told her father that they were meeting that evening, and he had indicated that he might just turn up whilst they were there. Sure enough, Mr Morris arrived about an hour later, and sat at the table with them. There was no small talk, he just launched into his first question. "Now, young Charles, just what are your intentions, lad?"

Charles took a deep breath and a few seconds to think. He then told Mr Morris that he wanted to marry Mary. Furthermore, that he had mentioned this to his mother, who had asked him to be sure to invite Mary round to our flat one evening for a talk.

Mr Morris smiled, and said, "I am glad to hear that. Now you will not be surprised to hear that Mrs Morris would like you to come round to our flat for tea on Sunday." He was obviously enjoying the situation, and before Charles could says anything he continued, "You are no doubt fully aware that I have made a lot of enquiries about you and your past associates, and will want some straight answers."

Charles nodded in agreement, and said, "You will get your answers, sir, but they may not be quite what you expect." He then promised to be at the Morris' home at four on the coming Sunday afternoon. Mr Morris then shook hands with him, and wished Charles and Mary good luck before departing.

Mary arrived at the Burton flat in good time on Saturday afternoon, and made a good impression on Mrs Burton. Mary mentioned that she had told her father that she and Charles wanted to get married, and that his reply had been to invite Charles to their home on the following day, Sunday, and he would pass judgement on him. But Mary insisted that irrespective of what her father might say, they had now decided that the best thing for them both was to get married anyway, in due time.

Mrs Burton said very little, but it was quite clear from her attitude that she was in full agreement with what Mary had said. Her final words were to remind them both how important it was that they both received the blessing of their parents, and that they had her blessing.

Next day, Charles was a little uneasy on his walk to the Morris' home. He had no idea how much Jim Morris actually knew about his previous activities, or the activities of his former colleagues in crime. Furthermore, as he had made the break from them, he had no intention of enlarging on his knowledge, whatever it might be.

On arrival, he received a warm welcome in the form of a typical British afternoon tea and cakes. The cross chat was real homely, and Charles was completely relaxed.

Then it happened! Jim Morris opened up the line of approach that had worried Charles ever since he had been invited. "Now, young Charles, just what is your connection with Jim Baker and his mates?"

"Well sir," he replied, "Jim and I were at school together, as was Mary, and we used to meet at Tony's regularly."

"Yes, yes, yes, I know all about that," said Jim Morris, "but why suddenly cut off the friendship? Come on Charlie, there's more to it than that, isn't there?"

Charles felt like the fish wriggling on the angler's hook. He had to say something, but he was not going to veer from the path of rectitude that he had decided upon when he ended his short life of crime. So he told Mr Morris of the times when he had gone out with Jim Baker to Boltons Store, and how Jim had shown him how to steal from shop counters. Also that he had seen Jim arrested by store detectives and had decided then that he was not going to get further involved in matters criminal.

It was the next step that worried him - telling Mr Morris about his introduction to Peter Ginsberg, a motor dealer, which had resulted in Peter teaching Charles how to drive his motor car. Charles had been so pleased and grateful, he confided, because he had always wanted to become a heavy goods driver like his father, and this was the first step in that direction, as driving lessons were something he knew his mother could never afford. He got on well with his driving, and on one occasion was taken to Tooley Street, over Tower Bridge, and asked to drive one of Peter's vehicles back to their yard in Back Church Lane. It was after this incident that he realised Peter had in fact done something to the ignition of the van whilst the driver was away. Furthermore, they had asked him to drive what was undoubtedly a stolen vehicle back to the yard for them.

The shock of that admission by his friend Jim Baker had gone a long way towards making Charles' mind up to cease his association with his two friends. Then, when his father's former boss Dan Jones, a regular visitor to the Burton home, had offered him a job as a van driver, he could see that his future was assured if he abandoned any further connections with his two friends.

Having ended his 'confession', Charles turned to Mr Morris, and said, "That is my story, sir. I have nothing further to add, except to say that I have had no further involvement with these people, and will not get involved with such matters again."

Jim Morris stood up and said, "I would like to think you have told me all the truth lad, but I have the feeling there must be more to it."

But Charles steadfastly denied that there was more to add, or that he had taken any further criminal actions in connection with his two friends. He admitted meeting them on odd occasions at Tony's café, but those meetings were coincidental, and there was no more to it than that.

Thankfully, the meeting developed into normal small talk after that session. Finally, Jim Morris announced that as far as he was concerned, there was no evidence that Charles had been further involved in criminal activity. He knew that he was highly respected by his boss Dan Jones, and added that Charles was lucky to have been strong willed enough to cut off his criminal connections completely before it was too late. His last words on the subject were, "Yes, young man, you can marry my daughter, but please remain steadfast in your vow never to get involved in criminal activity again. I wish you both every good fortune, but I will be watching over you both to ensure your wellbeing hereafter."

Charles and Mary married shortly after that interview. They have remained together happily ever since. Charles became a partner with Dan Jones in his haulage business, and remained ever thankful that he had seen the light in those early days. In fact, there were many times during his married life when he would return after a long journey and sit back and look at the ceiling, considering his good fortune in cutting himself loose from the bonds of crime completely. Such thoughts made him very happy on his own account, but pitiful of youngsters who, like him, would be led into a life of crime quite innocently, as he had been so led shortly after leaving school.